Roll Call

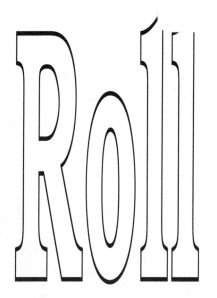

Overwhelmed by personal tragedy, John has no time for God, much less a "religious fanatic" for a student teacher. Can he find hope and healing before it is too late?

Roll Call

Overwhelmed by personal tragedy, John has no time for God, much less a "religious fanatic" for a student teacher. Can he find hope and healing before it is too late?

Carol Dixon

Roll Call

by Carol Dixon

©1995, Word Aflame Press
Hazelwood, MO 63042-2299

Cover design by Paul Povolni
Cover art by Art Kirchhoff

All Scripture quotations in this book are from the King James Version of the Bible unless otherwise identified.

All rights reserved. No portion of this publication may be reproduced, stored in an electronic system, or transmitted in any form or by any means, electronic, mechanical, photocopy, recording, or otherwise, without the prior permission of Word Aflame Press. Brief quotations may be used in literary reviews.

Printed in United States of America.

Printed by

Library of Congress Cataloging-in-Publication Data

Dixon, Carol
    Roll Call: novel / by Carol Dixon.
      p. cm.
    ISBN 1-56722-138-6
    1. Teachers—Fiction. I. Title.
    PS3554.I868R65   1995
    813'.54—dc20   95-33242
                                                                                   CIP

This book is lovingly dedicated
To my parents,

Ann and Karl Brooks,

Who instilled in me the joy of learning.

1

You are a soft formless slug, Mr. John Allan thought to himself. Looking across to the young man before him, he added mentally, Your parents found you under a cabbage leaf.

He hid his thoughts behind his usual professional demeanor. The teenager sitting on the other side of the desk imagined he had his teacher's rapt attention. As the boy continued his whining arguments he truly believed he was making some headway. He went on another five minutes, using the same grating tones that worked so well with his indulgent parents.

"No, David," Mr. Allan finally said in a tone of great patience. "You know all grades are predicated on a point system. I can't give you a passing grade if you don't have seventy-three points." You infant slug, he added silently.

Pouting as if he were five and not sixteen, David slunk from the room. His departure left Mr. Allan alone in the large public schoolroom. He sighed as he looked down at his grade book and saw the many zeros that followed David's name, like eggs in a carton.

John looked across to the peeling lime green walls that no one cared enough about to paint. He saw the old desks and textbooks that no one cared enough about to replace. He knew he only had to look up to see a sagging plaster ceiling that no one cared enough about to fix. Maybe David was right.

He felt the familiar despair settle over him like a blanket. Standing, he straightened his tie and buttoned his jacket.

Mr. John Allan, a literature and English teacher of Glendale High School, loved his job but hated the conditions he was forced to work in. He wasn't a very large man; in fact, most of his students towered over him. Yet discipline was never a real problem. He had what the Glendale students respectfully called "The Voice." It started somewhere around his shoe leather. From there it would work its way up until terrifically low majestic tones would proceed from his mouth. He could make "class dismissed" sound like an edict from God.

He liked to look as neat as possible, thinking it was a part of his work to set an example. He always wore a tie, with only the hottest days forcing him to take off his jacket. Though only forty, he had precious little hair left. It looked appropriate on him, though, as if an excess of hair would have been too frivolous.

With the exception of his eyes, one would have said he was a plain man. All his powers of attraction had gone into his voice and his eyes, as if his genes had wanted to concentrate their energies. His eyes were truly beautiful. A clear hazel color, with a double row of black lashes, his eyes held a world of warmth and good humor that often comes from working with young people.

David had taken up a good deal of his lunch period, so John decided to walk down to the teacher's lounge and just grab a cup of coffee. As he left his classroom, he noticed for the hundredth time the dull, mismatched linoleum on the floor. He carefully stepped around the places where there wasn't any linoleum at all.

The school simply had no money. Attempts to pass a levy had failed. John had often wondered in a school of over a thousand students if there weren't any parents who were carpenters or electricians or painters who would be willing to donate their time. Apparently, they didn't care either.

Upon reaching the teacher's lounge, he was met by the usual wave of cigarette smoke at the door. He grimaced and went in.

"Ah, John's down from his ivory tower," one of the teachers called from across the room.

"I needed a cup of coffee. I've been trying to explain to that Martin kid that ten times zero doesn't equal a passing grade."

"Oh, John. You're so funny," a female voice said a little too eagerly.

John winced and turned slowly. He hadn't seen Renee Grayson when he first walked in. There she was in all her glory, sitting on the large, beat-up couch in the corner. She smiled ingratiatingly while he poured himself a cup of coffee. When he was finished, she patted the empty space beside her.

"Here," she beckoned. "Come, sit by me."

He paused for a heartbeat, then noting there were only ten minutes left to his next class, he sat down.

"Thank you," he said smoothly, as he busied himself with his cup.

Miss Renee Grayson was the school's speech and drama teacher. It was a job John thought fitted her perfectly, as she seemed to be acting all the time. She was a short, blond woman, given to wearing enough makeup that she could have been seen several rows back in a very dark theater. She had a passion for flamboyant clothing, especially scarves that whipped about her neck and shoulders. He suspected she would have held a cigarette in a long black holder, if she could have gotten away with it.

He had somehow managed to fascinate her, though two people couldn't be more dissimilar. He wouldn't hurt her feelings for the world, but there was something about her that was too loud, too hard for him. Despite her smarminess around him, he had often heard her strident voice in the hallways, berating her students. That put him off more than anything.

She, on the other hand, thought they were perfect for each other: two cultured denizens of the arts. She perceived his formality with her as a symptom of shyness, something she was sure she could overcome.

"John, I've missed you at the Teacher's Union meetings," she said in what she imagined were soft tones. "We have to do more than just pay dues to be good members, you know."

John couldn't help but wince again. Renee had been teaching students to project their voices for so long, she didn't realize her own voice now made others want to project out of the room.

John looked into the depths of his coffee but found no answers there. For someone who was supposed to be so articulate, he was always strangely tongue-tied around Renee.

"I've been busy." It sounded lame in his own ears.

"Tomorrow is Saturday, so I know you don't have to spend all night grading papers."

"Well . . . no, but . . ." His mind refused to help him.

"No buts about it, dear. There's a meeting tonight. We could go together! What time should I pick you up?"

John noticed the room had become very quiet. The other teachers were making a great show of picking at their lunches or flipping through magazines. He knew, though, every ear was trained on this conversation. There was a look of desperation in Renee's eyes that he found touching. Her big mouth had placed her in a position of being publicly rejected by John, something he was loath to do.

The man who held a master's degree in English said, "Uh . . . well . . . I don't . . . I dunno . . ."

"Six-thirty? Great. See you then." Giving his arm a little pat, which happened to make him spill his coffee, she left, trailing her scarf and a cloud of perfume.

He stared at the growing brown stain on his pants leg for a moment, then looked up to see a paper towel being shoved at him. It was being offered by Steve Brooks, the gym teacher.

"I see you've been Graysoned," Brooks said with a grin, then sat down beside him on the couch.

"Graysoned?" John asked after he had taken the paper towel and begun to daub at his leg.

"Yeah, Graysoned is when she gets you to do something you don't really want to do."

"Oh. I didn't . . ." John lowered his voice to a whisper. "I didn't want to embarrass her in front of everyone."

"Embarrassed?" Brooks laughed and gave John a bone-rattling slap on the back, causing him to spill some more coffee. "She's as sensitive as a communal toothbrush. I saw those eyes she was giving you. Don't forget, John boy, she teaches acting."

John sighed. He looked up at the tall, athletic man beside him on the couch. He shook his head.

"You're right. I just couldn't think of a way out gracefully."

"You can't be graceful with Renee. First, you hit her between the eyes with a wet towel, then you carefully enunciate the word 'no.'"

"Enunciate—I like that Steve."

"Yeah, yeah, us jocks can talk good too. Now don't change the subject. You're letting that two-bit Betty Davis take advantage of you."

"Yes, love's plaything, that's me. Much as I appreciate your sympathy, I have a class starting in five minutes. Can you condense this lecture?"

"I could, but you still wouldn't listen. Have fun at the meeting tonight, John darling." Brooks batted his eyelashes and delicately lifted a hand to his brow.

John took advantage of his unguarded midsection and whacked him a hard one in the stomach.

"Oof! The truth hurts, eh John boy?" Brooks grimaced good-naturedly.

"You seem to be the one in pain," John dryly observed. He straightened his tie, then rose from the couch. "Adieu, mon ami."

John had an afternoon of oral book reports to listen to. These were often long stretches of half-done, last-minute efforts sprinkled with excuses. They could be an agony of boredom for him, but he felt they at least exposed the students to books, though he seriously doubted much reading was being done.

He sat ramrod straight at his desk, while a student did a very creative report on *David Copperfield* by Charles Dickens. It was so creative, in fact, he scarcely recognized the book.

John's lips twitched as the student wound up his report. He stopped the student before he sat down. "Chris, are you quite sure you read this book carefully?"

"Uh yeah, why?"

"I don't seem to recall the part you mentioned. About David performing magic for Queen Victoria?"

Chris had the grace to look embarrassed.

John shook his head, then motioned for Chris to be seated.

"David Martin, you're next."

"I didn't know book reports were due today," he said, his voice ending in a whine.

I will pour salt on you and make you shrivel up, you great white slug, John thought to himself. Your parents will wonder where you are, and I will point to the slick spot at your desk.

John put another zero in his grade book. Another egg in the crate, he thought to himself.

"Clark Nelson, you're next." John sat composedly, the picture of an interested listener. Actually he was making up his grocery list.

Clark was a tall, thin boy who had made trips to the barber into an art form. Today, his hair was shaved off except for a thick patch on top. One lock of hair had been braided and beaded and hung into his eyes.

John had labeled him as trouble when he'd first stepped into his classroom. There'd been a lot of rumors among the students that he was a drug user, maybe even a dealer. But the boy had never given John the least sign of it. In fact, Clark was one of his better students. He was really a quiet, studious boy with a quirky sense of humor. John had hoped to channel Clark into some creative but healthy outlets.

Today Clark stood in front of the class, his shirt tail half out, his pants pulled low as the current fashion dictated. He smiled slowly out of one side of his mouth.

"My book report is on *Goldilocks and the Three Bears*," he announced calmly.

John felt himself getting frustrated. He didn't make these assignments just to have them thrown in his face.

Before he could protest, though, Clark launched into a truly entertaining account of the old fairy tale. He did a perfect impression of Rush Limbaugh as the papa bear and Hillary Clinton as the mama bear. He managed to turn the old fairy tale into an astute political allegory. He also made some really terrible puns. John was delighted.

The class laughed a good five minutes after Clark had sat down.

After the students had been dismissed for the day, John stayed at his desk working on his grade book. A motion caught his eye and he looked up to see Steve Brooks standing in the doorway.

"Come to finish your lecture, Steve?"

"Nah, if you want to get tangled up in Renee's silken scarves, there's not much I can do about it."

"Oh, please."

The two men had been friends for years. John provided a calming balance to Steve's hyperactive personality.

Steve Brooks was an absolute fountain of energy. He could outdo any teenage boy in gym class. He could outrun, outjump any student that he had. His mind was nearly as active as his body. He was keenly interested in everything. He could have taught nearly any subject in the school, if he only could have sat still long enough.

He bent his sharp eyes towards John's grade book. "Any casualties? Anyone going down in flames?" he asked pointing at the book.

"It's just the first of October, Steve. We've hardly started."

"Don't play coy with me, John. I've got a basketball team to think of. I need fresh meat. There's a new school policy that says if you don't cut the mustard on the first report card, you're out of it for nine weeks. Nine weeks! That's a big slab of the season."

"Fresh meat? Mustard? Are you hungry or something?"

"Hardy-har. No, I've just got my eyes on this bruising hulk to be our new center this year, and I've got an awful feeling he's a few fries short of a Happy Meal."

"Now, you're making me hungry."

Steve sat down on a corner of the large wooden desk. He immediately began swinging his leg in a nervous fashion. John ignored him and continued to average grades.

"I can't stand it. I've got to know," Steve said after a pause of sixty seconds. "David Martin is the best student you've ever had, right?"

John slowly looked up from his grade book.

"Okay, okay," Steve said desperately. "He's not the best, but he's got the most potential?"

John frowned.

"So he doesn't have the most potential, but he tries really hard?" Steve asked, all hope dying.

John rolled his eyes.

"Can he spell his name?" Steve whispered dramatically.

John closed his grade book with a snap.

Steve moaned and buried his face in his hands. After a moment he looked up. "I knew it. I knew it was too good to be true. Couldn't his glands have left just a little bit for his brains?"

"There's nothing wrong with the boy's brains. It's his attitude. His parents have spoon-fed him for so long, he doesn't know how to do anything that requires any effort."

"Hmm, isn't this the part where the big, bad coach threatens the sincere, dedicated English teacher into giving his star player passing grades?"

"I hate cliches."

"Yeah, me too," Steve said as he got up from the desk and stretched. "Well, I guess it's just going to be another losing season with Central High getting the tournament."

"This is October. Shouldn't you wait for the season to start before you give up? Besides, what about Clark Nelson? He's as tall as David. He looks like he'd be lighter on his feet, anyway."

"That kid with the hair?" Steve wrinkled his nose. "Isn't he a troublemaker?"

"I'm surprised at you. After all your years of teaching, don't you know not to judge a student by how he looks?" John stood up too and began to fill his briefcase with work for home.

"It always works for me."

"It usually works for me too," admitted John with a smile. "Clark's different though. He's a very nice young man. Different, but nice."

The two men walked towards the door. As they

reached the hallway, Steve tripped on a piece of linoleum. He just managed to catch himself before he fell.

"Wow! Does maintenance know about these booby traps outside your door?"

"Yes, I've told them. I've told the principal. They say we don't have the money to fix the floor."

"So how are we going to pay for the lawsuit when some kid falls and his parents sue the school?"

"Maybe the superintendent or his two assistants will donate some of their pocket change," John said shrugging.

"Yeah, right," Steve replied as the two men left the building for the evening.

2

John drove up to a small beige house with a fenced-in yard. He had erected the fence over fifteen years ago to provide a safe enclosure for the children he had hoped to have. He had scarcely finished the job, though, before he had lost his young wife in a car accident. She had been pregnant with their first child.

He had worked through a lot of anger and grief in fifteen years. Time had worn away most of his hard edges. He had poured himself into his work, caring for and loving his students. His life revolved around other people's children.

There was one thing he had never resolved. His wife had been deeply religious. She had nearly brought him around to her way of thinking when the accident occurred. After that, John had tightly closed the door to his soul. He was furious at God.

He opened the gate to his yard and walked in. He could hear his dog barking before he got the door opened. As he took out his key, the dog became frantic at the jingling noise. At least someone is glad to see me, he thought to himself.

After he finally had the door open, twenty-five pounds of wheat-colored fur jumped up on him.

"That's right, Teddy. I'm wearing the black dress pants today. Let's see how much hair you can get on them."

John had always been disgusted by people who made a big fuss over their pets and talked baby talk to them. He didn't realize just how much he spoiled his own four-year-old cockapoo. He did manage to speak in sensible tones to it, though he spoke to it constantly.

As the phone had begun to ring, he let Teddy out into the yard while he went to the kitchen. When he picked up the receiver from the kitchen wall phone he was immediately sorry.

"John, dear!" Renee cooed across the line. He hated it when people said "John, dear." It made him feel like a piece of farm equipment.

"Yes, Renee?" You're calling to cancel, right? he thought frantically to himself.

"I was just thinking, we both have to eat, why don't I pick you up early. We could grab a couple of sandwiches on the way to the meeting."

She wants to make this into a date. This is not a date. We are two colleagues going to a professional meeting, he told himself, but he couldn't think of what to say to Renee.

There was a long pause as he thought.

"Well, John, if you really don't want to." She was pushing the guilt right through the telephone lines.

"No, no. It's not that I don't want to. It's four thirty now, and I was just wondering how much time I'd have to get ready." I sound like one of my girl students, he fumed.

"Oh, don't worry about that. It's just a casual meeting. I'll see you at five-thirty!" She hung up the phone.

"Renee. I don't want to go to this dumb meeting. You're pushing me and I don't like pushy women! I'm going to take a shower, then I'm going to take my dog for a walk!" he said firmly. Then he sighed and hung up the phone. He walked to his bedroom, where he began to get ready for the meeting.

At five-thirty sharp, Renee was parked in front of his house honking the car's horn.

Teddy looked up from where he was lying on the rug. John sighed and got up from the chair he'd been sitting in. "Well, Ted, that's my date. I know I shouldn't run for anyone who just honks the horn, but her intentions are honorable." He thought a moment as he gave the bushy dog a pat. "At least I hope they're honorable. I promise not to stay out late."

Ted looked at him with compassion, then lowered his head to his paws.

"Good night, old boy," John said as he went out the door.

Renee was sitting behind the wheel of a bright red sports car. She came from a very wealthy family. They made sure her lifestyle wasn't encumbered by her teacher's salary. At thirty, she was still very much a Daddy's girl.

When John opened the passenger door, his nostrils were assaulted by a heavy musk perfume. He blinked his eyes as he sank into the thickly padded, white leather seat.

"John, you look so nice," Renee said brightly as she patted him on the knee.

"This old thing?" he demurred. Keep your hands to yourself; you didn't even buy me a corsage. He told her off in his mind.

"Did I make a happy mistake!" she announced as she smoothly pulled the car into the street. "The meeting isn't until eight o'clock. We have plenty of time for dinner."

He smiled weakly.

"How about Da Vinci's? They've just remodeled. It's so beautiful and it's right across the bridge. Okay?" she asked.

John patted his pocket, to make sure his wallet was

still there. Thirty dollars, two credit cards . . . he began to make mental calculations.

"That sounds fine," he said calmly. "I haven't been there since they were just a pizza parlor."

"That was a long time ago! They're practically a four-star restaurant now."

I have my checkbook on me. I'm ahead on the water bill, so this could come out of the utility budget, he consoled himself.

"Great. I don't eat out much. This will be a treat," he commented.

"Have you ever done any acting, John?" she asked as they left his street.

"Funny you should ask that. Why?"

"It's your voice. You have the most thrilling low tones I've ever heard."

"Oh, I bet you say that to all the boys."

She laughed much too loudly for such a little joke. The small enclosure of the car couldn't contain her harsh, braying noise. John wanted to roll down a window to let out some of her laughter.

They were nearly to the bridge before she felt she had done proper homage to his humor.

"Really, John. For such a quiet man, you are just too, too much." She patted him on the knee again, this time letting her hand linger for a moment.

He shifted uncomfortably in his seat. She noticed his discomfort but attributed it to his supposed shyness. They were both silent until the car crossed the bridge and entered the restaurant's parking lot. John had an absurd fear that if he didn't hurry and get out of the car she would cross over and open his door for him.

They were hardly in the restaurant's lobby before Renee spotted some people she knew. She smiled broadly and grabbed John's arm possessively. He looked down in amazement at the vise grip she had on his arm.

"Ooh. There are some friends of mine from the community theater." She waved with her free hand while still clutching John's arm. "You don't mind if we go over and say hello, do you?"

Still surprised, John barely had time to nod his head before he found himself being propelled across the room. They approached a couple sitting at one of the white-clothed tables in the middle of the room. They were a nice-looking pair who seemed to be very normal, even if they were friends of Renee.

"Kerry and Jeanna. It's so good to see you!" she said loudly. "I haven't had a chance to tell you how much I loved that play last week." She turned to John, "They both did 'The Hollow' at the theater. It was wonderful. Agatha Christie would have been so proud."

The man named Kerry looked as if he were going to make a comment, but Renee rushed on. "I want you to meet . . ." she paused as if at a loss for words, "I want you to meet a really special friend of mine, John."

John didn't like the way she had stressed "special." He especially didn't like the way her hand was tightened around his arm like a blood-pressure cuff. His fingers were tingling.

The man named Kerry had deep amber eyes that looked at John with understanding. He knew Renee very well. He nodded at John. "Nice to meet you."

"Thank you. Renee and I just work together," John said pointedly.

"Well, we'll let you eat now. Bye, bye." Renee gave a friendly wave, though there was fire in her eyes. They walked back to the waiting hostess, then to the table she had selected for them.

Renee was silent while she fought to regain her composure. She really had a bad temper, though she had always taken great pains to hide it when she was around John. Being single and thirty ate at her. As her dating life was pretty dismal, it had meant a lot to her to have acquaintances see her out with a man. She wondered how much the couple had made of John's remark.

John was feeling pretty guilty. He hadn't wanted to embarrass Renee, but they were definitely not a couple. He didn't appreciate her trying to pass them off as one. He felt a large part of Renee's attraction to him was simply because he was unmarried and presentable. If another single man with prospects were to come along she'd be sure to go after him with the same fervor.

The silence continued as the two glanced over their menus. John saw they had remodeled the prices as well as the restaurant's interior.

Presently, Renee began to brighten again and tried to make a stab at conversation. "You know we'll be meeting our student teachers Monday night?"

"Yes. I'm looking forward to it," John replied pleasantly.

Renee peeped over her menu at him and whispered theatrically. "I was able to find out all about your new protégé. Interested?"

Surprised, John raised his eyebrows, "What do you mean?"

"Oh, John. You really got the luck of the draw. One of my friends at the college knows your student teacher. His name is Fred Evans."

"What do you mean, Renee? Luck of the draw?"

She smirked and reached across with her vermilion-tipped nails to lower the menu he was holding up. "Poor Johnny. They've hooked you up with the biggest religious fanatic on campus. A real live holy roller. He's Pentecostal. He'll probably try to convert your students and speak in tongues in the classroom."

John froze, staring at her. Seeing that she had chained his interest, she began to wax on about Pentecostals in general. After she had told a very old and stale joke about them, John shut his menu and looked down at the tablecloth.

"My late wife was a Pentecostal," he said stiffly.

Renee was saved from any response by the approach of the waitress. For an awful moment, Renee was afraid John would get up and leave her sitting in the restaurant. He only ordered quietly, never looking up from the table.

After the waitress had left, Renee reached across to place her hand on John's. "John, I'm so, so sorry. I didn't know."

John retrieved his hand and placed it in his lap. Renee had managed to dig up something he had believed was long buried. He didn't feel like placating her anymore. "You are certainly entitled to your opinions."

The meal was uncomfortable. Renee was very subdued, trying to think of how to make up for her gaffe. John could only think of the young man who was coming into his life. He wondered if he could be half as zealous as Renee made out. In any case, the boy had better not try to convert him. John would certainly have something to say about that.

John saw pouting on a daily basis in his classroom; he was not about to be accused of such immature behavior himself. He rallied his manners enough to be civil and polite to Renee as they finished the meal and left for the meeting. But he was making it clearer than he ever had before that they were only co-workers.

Glendale was a very small town. The city could be crossed in less than twenty minutes, so the ride from the restaurant to the meeting was mercifully brief.

John wondered idly what the meeting was about. When he'd first started teaching, he'd been glad for the union. It was nice to have some measure of security in his line of work. Plus, the union had worked for better wages and benefits.

However, as the years had worn on, he felt the union was becoming more and more political. The union leaned heavily to the left, espousing causes he didn't believe in.

The last meeting he had attended was over a year ago, when a speaker spent an hour telling the teachers how to vote in the upcoming elections. The speaker had ended the tirade by saying anyone who voted for a certain party should quit teaching as they were anti-education. Since the party in question was the one John had belonged to all his voting life, he decided not to attend any more union meetings.

He was faithful in his dues, though. He had heard of too many nonunion teachers being frozen out of their jobs. He disagreed with the union, but he felt it would be career suicide to say so.

That night's meeting was being held in a rented hall. John noted there were out-of-town license plates on some of the cars. They must have brought in the big guns, he thought to himself.

As they entered the hall, Renee stuck close to John's side. She didn't try to take his arm, however, for which he was very grateful. There were plenty of familiar faces from different schools in the area, but there were four people near the podium that he had never seen before.

The quartet was conversing intently with the local union president, Shirley Caedmon. John had only a nodding acquaintance with Ms. Caedmon, but he knew she took her union duties very seriously. She took an aggressive stance with the community as a whole. She believed only professional educators could know what was best for the schools. Parents should only provide the necessary students for teaching and school boards should help generate the funding. Period. Her hard line had caused a lot of friction in the last few years, especially with the Glendale school board.

Spotting two empty chairs, Renee and John walked over and sat down. John gave Renee the aisle seat on his left, then noticed with delight that Grace Burton was seated to his right.

"Mrs. Burton. What a pleasure! How are you?" he asked the delicate, white-haired woman who was beaming up at him.

"Little Johnny. Oh, dear. Well, I guess you aren't so little are you?" she laughed. "How long has it been?" She took his outstretched hand into her two tiny hands.

"I'm just flattered you remember me."

"Why, Johnny, how could I forget you? You were always asking questions in my class. Drinking in everything I said with those huge eyes of yours," she smiled impishly, "Of course, you did have a little more hair then."

He laughed good-naturedly and passed a hand over his bald pate. He then felt Renee's presence hovering over his left shoulder. He sighed to himself then turned towards her.

"Renee, this is Mrs. Grace Burton. She was my high school English teacher."

Renee was all smiles. She leaned heavily against John as she reached out to shake the older woman's hand.

"Mrs. Burton, this is Ms. Renee Grayson. She and I teach together at Glendale High."

"Delighted, my dear."

They wanted to talk more, but Ms. Caedmon was approaching the lectern on the podium.

"We'll talk after the meeting, Johnny," Mrs. Burton whispered as she affectionately patted John's hand.

John nodded, feeling better than he had in hours. High school had been a difficult time for him. He had been quite shy and studious. Mrs. Burton's English class had been one of the highlights of those awkward years. He had responded to her kindness long before he became interested in what she was teaching.

She'd always seem to sense when a student was having a bad day. She'd then talk just a little bit softer to them. Encourage them in some small way.

As the minutes from the last meeting were being read, John continued to reminisce about his high school days, when he had first become interested in teaching. His mind wandered for some minutes as necessary business was being discussed from the podium. Then Ms. Caedmon said the one word that could snap him back to attention.

"Strike!"

John blinked. Mrs. Burton let out a small gasp of dismay. Ms. Caedmon smiled grimly, pleased that she now had everyone's attention. She had grasped both sides of the metal lectern and was leaning forward. Dressed in a trim red suit, she looked quite competent and professional, even a little intimidating.

"It's an ugly word, isn't it?" she asked the quiet crowd. "No one wants to hear it. No one wants to say it." She pointed a well-manicured finger at the assembled teachers. "Absolutely none of us wants to do it!"

She slowly walked to one side of the lectern and folded her arms. Sweeping the room with a glance that included everyone, she continued. "Yet we continue to be underpaid and overworked. We have as much training if not more than other professionals. Some of you in this room have master's degrees, even doctorates. Do any of us make as much as a doctor? No. Teachers are the only white-collar workers who are treated like blue-collar workers."

"When the levy failed to pass, the community told us what it thought. The community told us the value it placed on education. Perhaps we should tell the community what we think."

She went on for some time pointing out what was wrong, what was lacking. Then, one by one, she introduced the people behind her, all union officials on the state level.

Each of these officials expounded at some length about the transgressions that the community was committing against the teachers. They then began to discuss the various options that the teachers had. Every speech ended on the same note: a strike.

John's dismay increased with each word. So much of what they said was right. So much was totally true. He was vastly underpaid for his experience and education. He did have pathetic working conditions. Then why wasn't he as dissatisfied as these people obviously were?

The floor was opened up for discussion. A great deal was said pro and con concerning a strike. John sat quietly through it all. He was amazed at how strong the feelings ran.

A final referendum would not be taken that night, but the school board would be notified of the possibility of a strike. John could not believe there was even a possibility.

The meeting was finally adjourned. John just sat for a moment taking everything in. Even Renee seemed thoughtful.

"A strike!" she said, "How awful."

John shook his head in agreement, then turned to Mrs. Burton. "Did you think it was this bad? Bad enough to strike for?" he asked her gently.

"I don't know, Johnny. When I started teaching things were so different. Better in some ways, worse in others." She looked up at him with her pale blue eyes. "I just don't know."

3

There was something about Mondays. The students didn't really walk into class on Monday mornings. They oozed in, like thick molasses poured from the bottle. Their forward motion was the result of gravity alone.

Some students didn't "do" Mondays at all. They labored under the misconception that the weekend consisted of three days, not two. As John Allan stood taking the roll that morning, he had already marked David Martin absent when the young man walked in the door.

John raised his eyebrows as David slouched into the room, then slumped down in his seat.

"Hey! All visitors gotta sign in at the office!" Karen, the girl behind David, called out.

"Yeah, is this our new student teacher, Mr. Allan?" Clark Nelson asked. "He looks just like David Martin, only David would never be here on a Monday."

"You're so funny, Clark," David sneered, "You oughta train this dog behind me and start a circus act."

Karen hit David over the head with her grammar book. Instantly David began to whine. "She hit me! Did you see that, Mr. Allan?"

"See what, David?" John calmly asked. I paid her big money to do that, he thought to himself.

"Open your grammar books to page 102, class," John instructed, cutting off David in mid whine. "We will be starting a new unit today on using comparative and superlative degrees of irregular modifiers."

Groans went up all over the classroom.

The rest of the period was uneventful, save for the fact that David actually turned in his homework. As the class was filing out the door at the end of the period, Clark whispered to John as he was going past, "I don't want to scare you, Mr. Allan, but David was reading his textbook today!"

Cindy, another student, walking behind Clark, whispered, "Now don't panic, Mr. Allan, but I think David was . . ."—her eyes got bigger—"David was taking notes!"

John's clear hazel eyes danced with amusement while he kept his lips tightly closed. He never joked about one student to another, no matter how strong the temptation.

The warm October morning stretched into the afternoon. It was a drowsy type of day in which the students were too listless to cause any discipline problems but too sleepy to really learn anything—one of the uneasy tradeoffs John had learned to live with in twenty years of teaching.

As John prepared to lock up the classroom for the evening, Steve Brooks walked in the door.

"Steve, I missed you at lunch. Did you have a nice weekend?"

"Hey, that's my question to you. How was the BIG DATE?" he intoned dramatically.

"You're invited to the wedding. I'll name our first child after you."

"Even if it's a girl? Come on now, John boy, was spending an evening with Miss Broadway as bad as I can imagine it would be?"

"Worse."

"Eww, what'd she do? Tap dance in the restaurant? Organize the waiters into a chorus line?"

"With her usual tact and diplomacy, she managed to insult my late wife. No mean feat, considering Linda has been dead for fifteen years," John said quietly.

Steve was silent for a moment as he looked at his friend. His large blue eyes were full of compassion. He hadn't heard John mention his wife in a long time.

"I'm really sorry, John. What did she say?"

John only shook his head and buttoned his slate gray suit jacket. He ran a hand over the back of his head, smoothing down what remained of his hair. Steve saw that he was not going to answer his question.

"How do I look?" John asked.

"Impeccable. The consummate professional, a sartorial splendor," Steve answered. He sensed how badly John wanted to change the subject.

"Such a vocabulary, wasted on monosyllabled jocks."

"Bigot. So tell me, John, why the concern over your appearance?"

"We're supposed to meet our student teachers in an hour, remember? I thought I could at least look as if I knew what I was doing," John replied.

Steve pulled at his sweat shirt, then picked up his feet one at a time as he stared intently at his tennis shoes. "I'm ready," he announced.

John smiled warmly at the man who understood him so well. Their friendship worked because Steve knew not to press for confidences. John was intensely private despite his friendliness. The light, bantering tone they took with each other was important to him. It kept everything at arm's length.

"They have student teachers for gym class? I suppose you have to learn the correct way to blow a whistle?"

"You egghead. Gym teachers identify the developmental needs of individuals for motor, cognitive, and social skills. Then with the creative utilization of facilities and equipment we mold each student to his optimum level of functioning."

"How long did it take to memorize that?"

"Two days. Impressed?"

"Very." John slapped Steve on the shoulder and walked towards the door. "Come on, let's go meet these college kids."

The meeting was to be held in the cafeteria, which was in the large right wing of the building. It was located on the third floor, the same floor as John's classroom.

As always, the two men talked shop. They related the events of the day as they walked slowly towards the cafeteria.

"This was a red-letter day in Glendale history. David Martin came to school on a Monday, did his homework, and took notes in class," John said as he shook his head in wonder.

"You're welcome," Steve quipped.

"Excuse me?"

"Yes. You have moi to thank for little Davey boy's behavior. We had a heart-to-heart chat. I was able to motivate the lad to improve his scholastic achievements. Really, John, the boy just needs a little encouragement. You should try it some time."

"Ha! The boy just needs an attitude transplant. So tell me, did this little heart-to-heart chat involve basketball in anyway?"

"Mmm, could be."

"Well, whatever works," John said as they reached the cafeteria and opened the heavy glass and metal doors. "Still, it doesn't seem right, cajoling that pampered rich kid with basketball when I have so many other good students who work twice as hard."

"But they're such short good students."

John shot a baleful glance up at his much taller friend. "Watch it, buddy," he warned.

"Did I say short? I meant compact, uh . . . untall."

"That's it. One on one, tomorrow at four in the gym. Be there."

"You're on, O man of diminutive stature."

The large cafeteria was filling up with teachers, although the student teachers hadn't arrived yet.

"Give me some money, John, and I'll buy you a cup of coffee out of the machine. I hear the man came and changed the grounds just last month."

"Well, thanks. I suppose I have to buy yours too?" John asked.

Steve just smiled.

"Really, I don't see how your wife stands you," John grumbled as he dug in his pocket for some change.

"She adores me. Now go get us some seats."

John walked over to one of the large, long tables. He sat down at one end where there were still some empty seats. Across from him sat Calvin Loring, the computer teacher. Loring was talking to Maggie McCarty, another English teacher. Their faces were intent and serious. They turned to John as soon as he sat down.

"John, you were at the meeting. Do you think there'll be a strike?" Loring asked.

"I don't know. I hope not," he answered.

"Why? Don't you think it would be justified?" Loring's voice sounded irritated.

John was surprised at the man's tone. Before he could answer, he felt a hand on his shoulder. Simultaneously he caught a whiff of strong perfume. He knew who it was before he turned his head. "Renee," he smiled weakly.

"Oh, John, I just have to talk to you," she said as she sat down to his left. John could sense all conversation at his end of the table slamming to a halt. Much too loudly, Renee continued, "We were having such a wonderful time Friday night. I can't tell you what it meant to me. Then I had to go and spoil it all. You know I would never intentionally try to hurt you, John."

Several heads were averted from the pair, which just happened to put their ears in the best position. All the better to hear you with, my dear, John thought to himself.

"It's all right, Renee," John said in a low voice.

"No, I can tell you're still mad at me," she said a couple of decibels higher.

"I'm not mad," he ground out between his teeth.

She grabbed his upper arm convulsively, "I'm so glad! Now if you really mean that, you'll come to my house for dinner tomorrow night. I want to make up for spoiling our time at Da Vinci's."

"He's already spoken for, Renee." Steve Brooks had just walked up behind them. "The old man thinks he can take me at basketball. I won't let him use you to get out of it. Besides, my wife was planning a big dinner for us afterward."

Renee looked disappointed, then smiled as she gave John's arm a hard squeeze. "Oh, well there's always Wednesday night. We'll talk later, John. I promised some of the girls I'd sit at their table."

She stood and faced Steve, who was holding two steaming cups of coffee. "Why, thank you, Steve! How sweet," she said, as she took one of the cups and walked away.

"Uh . . uh . ." Steve spluttered. John reached up and deftly took the remaining cup from his hand. "Sit down, Steve, and quit gasping like a fish out of water."

"I really wanted some coffee," Steve pouted as he sat down.

"Caffeine is bad for hyperactive children like you. But thanks for saving my bacon. Now how are you going to explain this big dinner to your wife?"

"What's to explain? I said she was planning a big dinner; I didn't say she was going to cook it. You can just treat us to the great Da Vinci's afterward."

"Hardy-har. My budget's already blown for the month. Bring her over to my house; I'll fix us something."

"Ew, a bologna casserole? I've heard about you single guys."

"So, Steve, what's your opinion on this strike business?" It was Loring again.

Steve shook his head, suddenly serious. "I'm against it. I've got a family to support."

"As if you're supporting them now, on a teacher's salary," Loring said fretfully.

"A small wage is better than no wage at all. These strikes can go on for months."

"That's a pretty nearsighted view, isn't it? Is this what you went to college for? To make less money than some factory worker?"

"I went to college so I wouldn't have to work in a factory. Believe me, those people earn every dime they make," Steve returned.

"Are you saying we don't?" Loring was becoming angry. He was a large heavyset man who always seemed to be sweating. A thin line of perspiration was already forming on his flushed brow. He leaned aggressively across the table, his black eyes rock hard behind his thick glasses.

"I didn't say that." Steve refused to be baited. "Look, we live in a economically depressed community. Plants and businesses are closing down. I may not have it great, but I've got tenure. I'm working at a job that is almost recession proof. You'll have to excuse me if I don't feel like rocking the boat."

John was silent, watching the exchange.

"It's attitudes like yours that keep things the same. Do you know that I'm supposed to teach two hundred kids computer every week, on five computers? The Health teacher told me she was having to explain the complete respiratory system to students who don't have textbooks. It's impossible. The parents just don't care. How are we going to make them care without a strike?" Loring demanded.

"A lot of those parents are unemployed. How are they going to get excited about our wages and our working conditions when they don't have a job at all?"

35

Loring was prevented from answering by the arrival of the student teachers. A large group of nicely dressed young people were coming through the double doors, followed by the principal and a college professor. The doors were just swinging shut when a young man, obviously late and running to catch up, tried to slip in. The briefcase he was carrying slammed into the glass of the door. A large crash was heard as the briefcase shattered the glass. The collision snapped the clasp on the airborne briefcase, causing a flurry of white paper as the contents of the case were vomited out. After the first initial gasps of surprise, the whole room was deathly quiet as every eye trained on the young man. Each and every teacher there was studying his name badge to see if he belonged to them.

He was a tall, angular young man with a shock of thick blond hair that kept falling into his eyes as he bent to pick up his papers. He wore an ill-fitting polyester suit that showed too much of his bony wrists and ankles. He was wearing white socks and very large tennis shoes with his suit. He wasn't a bad looking young man, except for his extreme thinness and some acne that still troubled him.

For every five papers he retrieved, two seemed to fall from his hands. A couple of the student teachers took pity on him and tried to help him clean up. But for the most part, the student teachers were trying to act as if he wasn't there. The professor looked ill.

When he finally stood up, John leaned forward, intently studying the boy's name badge.

"Oh no," he whispered as he read, "Hello! My name is Fred Evans."

"My students will eat him alive," John whispered to Steve.

"He's yours? Are you sure?" Steve whispered back.

"Positive. I checked the sheet that was posted. Plus, Renee told me his name. She'd heard of him."

The men became quiet as the principal prepared to speak. He had been waiting for the glass from the door to be swept up by the janitor. The principal, James Gilman, looked dismally at the ruined door, wondering when, if ever, it would be fixed. He speared Fred Evans with a disapproving stare, then turned to face the room. He made a few comments, then allowed the student teachers and teachers to have a chance to meet each other.

John watched as Fred Evans craned his neck around, looking to be claimed. John sighed as he slowly pushed himself from the table.

"Jump on in; I'm sure the water's fine," Steve quipped.

"It's his briefcase I'm worried about," John said as the two men stood up. He carefully smoothed his lapels, then walked towards the young man.

"Fred Evans? I'm John Allan," John said as he approached.

Evans was painfully eager. He grasped John's hand and pumped it hard. "Hello! Mr. Allan, I'm so glad to meet you. I feel terrible about the door, of course, but I am glad to meet you. It's just great. Not the door, I mean."

Feeling slightly confused, John nodded and extracted his hand. He pointed to a couple of chairs and asked, "Would you like to sit down?"

When they were seated, John was nearly on eye level with the young man. All of his great height was in his legs. Evans perched forward on his folding chair, causing his knees to stick up at an awkward angle. He clutched his deadly briefcase across his lap, as if afraid it might get him into further trouble.

He had enormous pale blue eyes that were staring intently into John's face. He scrutinized John in silence for a few moments, then spoke in a rush. "All the other student teachers really envy me. Not because of me, I mean, but because of you. I don't mean that they envy you either. I mean they envy you because you have me. Oh! I didn't mean that! I mean they envy me because I have you as a supervising teacher. Do you see what I mean?"

John felt a headache coming on, the type of headache that settled right between the eyes and stayed for hours. He tried to smile. "Thank you. I'm sure that's very flattering."

"No really I meant it. I wasn't trying to flatter you. Not that I wouldn't compliment you or anything like that, but I like to say what I mean and I try to mean what I say," Evans said nervously.

Ten weeks, ten weeks, this boy will be in my classroom for ten weeks, John thought to himself. He felt as if he were beginning a prison sentence. "Well, Fred, I'm sure we'll get along just fine. Now, you'll need to be rather firm with my students. They're good kids, but they'll see how far they can push you. Especially at first."

"Firm, yes, all right." Evans nodded his head vigorously. "Tell me, do you use assertive discipline, reality therapy, or do you just follow Maslow's hierarchy?"

"Oh, I usually just hit them over the head with a two-by-four."

Evans blinked several times then said softly, "I thought corporal punishment wasn't allowed in this state."

"I was kidding, Fred."

"Oh, yes, yes, of course!" Evans blushed crimson, then made a feeble attempt at laughing. It was a sad effort, loud enough to cause several heads to turn their way.

John tried to explain his lesson plans to him, but he felt as if he wasn't really listening. Or rather, he was trying so hard to catch every word that the young man wasn't taking it in.

"Now, Fred, I teach four English grammar classes. The seniors and the ninth grade are never any real problem. The sophomores, though, you have to put them to work as soon as they get in the door."

"Why?"

"There's a couple of troublemakers in that group who will get everyone stirred up if they get a chance. So I found if I keep them busy there aren't any fights."

"Fights?" Evans gulped nervously.

"Yes. Brad and Gorden are a couple of real cases, trash talkers, firebugs—you know the type."

"Firebugs?" Evans asked weakly.

"Right. Now mind you, they've never started a fire on school property—that would be a permanent suspension. But a lot of rumors are floating around about what they do after school."

"I see, what about the eleventh grade?"

"Hmm, well . . . yes, the eleventh grade," John groped for the words that would be honest without being too frightening. "Very creative personalities, very dynamic . . ." Very creative about getting out of work, very dynamic about getting into trouble, John finished in his own mind. Sensing that he'd lulled Evans into a sense of security, he hurried on, "I also teach literature fifth, sixth, and seventh periods."

"Don't you have a planning period?"

"Yes," John smiled, "From three-thirty to eleven every night." John didn't tell him that as a senior teacher he could have two planning periods a day if he wished. Shortly after his wife had died, John had learned that staying busy was the best way to stay sane.

John felt a great deal of sympathy for the nervous young man sitting across from him. When he thought of all that lay in store for Evans in the next ten weeks, he concluded it was probably a good thing that the boy was a religious fanatic. He needed all the prayers he could get.

"I thought for the first few days it might be best if you just observed my classes. It would give you a chance to learn our routine."

Evans nodded with relief.

"Great! . . . uh I mean, what a great idea. Children work best with structure and I wouldn't want to destructure their structure."

John waited to see if he was kidding. He wasn't.

"Right. A word of warning, though: I wouldn't call them children to their faces. It wouldn't be healthy."

"Yes, all right. You're right, of course. Their self-esteem is very fragile at this stage of development. A loss of stature within their peer group could manifest itself. . . ."

John placed a polite smile on his face and wondered how much actual class time he would spend with this boy before the students killed him.

Between the threat of a strike and his new student teacher, John had a lot to think about that night as he drove home. His mind rested briefly on his conversation with Loring. It amazed him at how angry the man was. Judging from Friday night's meeting, a large group of people shared Loring's feelings. He wondered where it would all end.

As he reached home and opened the large glass storm door on the side porch, he thought of Fred Evans. He wondered where the boy was from. Glendale was a small town with only one Pentecostal church. The boy must surely attend the same church his wife had gone to.

He went upstairs to change for bed. As he undressed he thought of how fond his wife had been of her church. He stared at the old photo he kept on the dresser. The beautiful silver frame held the picture of a slender young woman. Her thick brown hair was swept up in the back. Her large brown eyes glinted with laughter. She had a dimple on each side of her wide smile.

She had only lived a year after she had joined the church. But how happy she had been! It seemed to John she had laughed all the time. He remembered the Sunday they had made her a Sunday school teacher. You'd have thought she'd been given a master's degree. She'd gone on and on about what an honor it was. She'd said what a privilege it was to be trusted with those wonderful children.

He hadn't understood. He'd only laughed at her enthusiasm. But he couldn't have dampened her spirits even if he had wanted to. She had spent that week planning for her Sunday school class.

Taking the picture in his hands, John sat down on his bed, a flood of memories washing over him. She would have started her maternity leave the following week. She had so looked forward to the extra time she would have to get ready for the baby, to work with her new Sunday school class and just to be with him.

The Saturday before she was to teach her first Sunday school session she had thought of one more poster she wanted to buy for the little basement classroom she'd been given. She'd begged John to take her down to the school supply store.

"You've already spent a fortune there!" he'd groused good-naturedly. "Besides, until you can wear your seat belt again, you shouldn't be in a car any more than necessary."

But she'd gotten her way as usual. He'd been so anxious when Linda had stopped wearing her seat belt because of the pregnancy. He had tried to get her to stay out of cars or at least ride in the back seat. She'd only laugh and tell him she was trusting in the Lord.

John had driven so carefully that day. He'd been stopped at a stop sign, waiting for a clear lane to enter the highway, when he heard a loud crash of ripping metal. He remembered seeing a blue patch of sky as their car was thrown to the left, then there was nothing.

He had awakened a day later in the hospital, surrounded by sad-faced nurses. A doctor had walked in at that point. One look at his face and John knew. He was a childless widower.

A drunk driver had come off the highway at seventy miles an hour and struck the left back end of the car. The resulting spin had sent his wife right out of the car. The doctors swore she had never known a thing. John wished he could believe that.

The days after didn't focus in his memory. He remembered a lot of kind, empty words and a lot of kind, blank faces. He had only one clear memory of those days. That memory he would carry to his grave. That memory had set his actions for the next fifteen years.

The day of the funeral, several of his wife's students had attended. Before the minister began, the children had shuffled past John as he sat on the front row. Some cried, some hugged him. But one little girl, her eyes huge and moist had taken his hand.

"Why, Mr. Allan? Why?" she had asked sorrowfully. John had had no answer for her but had only looked angrily at his wife's pastor. Full knowing he was being unfair, John had allowed all his bitter anger to focus on that one man. In the days ahead, John realized his rage was directed at the God the man represented.

The church members had reached out to him, the pastor had tried to counsel with him, but John had spurned every gesture of kindness. He wanted nothing to do with them or their God.

As he looked at the photo of his wife, he thought how unhappy she would be if she had known. John shook his head, but of course she couldn't know. She was gone for good.

He had thought he had shut the door on all his heartache. Now here was Fred Evans shattering that door just as surely as he'd shattered the glass door at school.

5

John always arrived at school a good half hour before the students. He liked to be prepared. He also liked the quiet. So he was a little surprised that Tuesday morning to see his classroom door open and all the lights on.

Curious, he looked in, hoping none of his students were doing something they shouldn't. He had a few rough teenagers that he wouldn't turn his back on. Not for a minute.

He was surprised to see it was Fred Evans. Sitting in the back, on a folding chair by a table, Fred had a Bible spread across his bony knees. His hands were clasped across the Bible. He was leaning forward with his eyes shut, obviously praying. John felt his surprise turn to anger.

"Just what do you think you're doing?" he demanded.

Startled, Fred jumped to his feet, knocking his Bible and chair to the floor in one motion. "Oh! I was just . . . I was just praying," he stammered.

"You do understand this is a public school? There must be a clear separation of church and state. No Bible studies or prayer meetings with the students?" John asked with asperity.

The boy reached over and picked up his Bible. John could see it was old and well-used. A few of its pages had come loose from the binding and were scattered on the floor. Fred collected the pages before he answered. His face was a bright red as he clutched the Bible to his chest.

"I understand this is a public school," Fred said quietly. "But I was nervous, this being my first day and all. I thought I'd come to class early and pray," he finished anxiously. "But just for myself; I'd have put my Bible in my briefcase before the students arrived."

John suddenly felt like a member of the Gestapo. What a way to treat a student teacher on his first day! John shook his head, Godzilla versus Bambi, he thought to himself.

"Fred, look I'm . . ." John started but he didn't get a chance to finish.

"Hey, John!" Steve Brooks called from the hallway. "Ready for ten weeks of student nerd?" Steve made quite a picture as he stood in the doorway, his face growing as red as the sweat shirt he was wearing. "So, John ready for the student herd?" he asked, making a lame attempt at a save.

"Mr. Allan, I think I have some papers to sign at the office," Fred said awkwardly as he excused himself from the room.

"I'm sorry, I'm sorry," Steve began to moan as he sat down heavily at a desk. "As if that kid won't be going through enough from the students."

"You don't know the half of it," John said as he walked to his desk at the front left corner of the room.

"It's the suit. Geez, where did he find a polyester leisure suit in a color that doesn't occur in nature?" Steve quipped.

"I thought you were sorry?" John asked.

"I am, I am. But it's like he was advertising it. 'I am a nerd. Amuse yourselves at my expense.'"

"Stop picking on my student teacher. I suppose yours is perfect?"

"Thad? He's a regular side of beef. He can bench-press a Volkswagon, but I don't think he could spell it. I'm sure all our female students will be in love with him before the day is over."

John laughed. "Besides demoralizing my student teacher, did you have a purpose to this early morning visit? I thought you always started your day off with a hundred laps in the gym."

Steve was suddenly serious. "Yeah, I was wondering if you'd heard. There's going to be an emergency levy placed before the town to generate funds for the schools. The talk is, if it's voted down the union is going to have us walk."

"You're not serious."

"I wish I wasn't, John. But this whole issue has reached the boiling point. The buildings are a mess, the textbooks need replacing, and we've all had a wage freeze for the last three years."

"But like you said last night, Steve, this whole valley is economically depressed. How are you going to pass a levy that will raise people's property taxes?"

"I know, but there are some hot heads in the union who insist on taking this whole levy business very personally."

"Like Loring?"

"Yeah, like Loring. How'd you like to face him on the picket line?"

"What do you mean, Steve? Would you cross the picket line?"

Steve stood up, looking guilty. The first bell rang, its echoes dying in the room before he answered. "My dad worked in the factories all his life. He belonged to three different unions. Those unions kept him safe, kept him working. I had it drilled into my brain how important union membership is. This seems so different. Our union is always pushing some liberal ideology. Do you know they have a whole platform on abortion?"

"I know," John said.

Steve walked to the doorway. Turning he said, "I've got a wife and two little kids. I've got to do what's best for them. You can't collect unemployment pay when you go on strike." Steve paused for a moment and looked at the floor, then he searched John's face. "I hope this won't hurt your opinion of me."

"What opinion?" John smiled, trying to lighten the moment. "Don't worry about it, Steve. We'll talk some more this afternoon . . . after I beat you at basketball."

Steve smiled and went out the door. "In your dreams!" he yelled from the hallway.

The morning passed uneventfully. After Fred was introduced, he stayed glued to the chair in the back. He was obviously too terrified to move. He reminded John of a deer caught in the headlights of a car.

The students could sense his fear. It caused a rustle of anticipation in the classroom. Veteran that John was, he knew what was up. The students were thinking of the high times that were ahead when John would leave this innocent in charge of the classroom. By noon, the word had spread throughout the school. The students' pack instincts were always right on target. Without saying one word, Fred had marked himself as easy prey.

As John dismissed the last class for lunch, he wondered how he could help Fred. Well, he decided, there were at least two weeks before he would really have to turn the classes over to him.

"Fred, would you like to go get some lunch now?" John prompted gently.

"What? Oh, sure." Fred broke from his reverie and stood up. He looked rather uncertainly at John for a moment, not sure what to do next.

John felt really bad. He'd always had a reputation as being the dream supervising teacher. College professors usually fought to get their pet student teachers placed with him. He'd been known for his patience and kind leadership.

He looked up into the boy's nervous face and realized that Fred was afraid of him. He knew he should apologize about his outburst that morning. He came very close. But something held him back.

The noise of the cafeteria could be heard several doors away. It was packed as always with masses of teenagers all wanting their lunch. There were long lines in front of five overworked vending machines. Fred sighed as he saw how far back the lines of students went.

Hearing the sigh, John looked up and smiled. "One of the few privileges of teaching, son . . . we don't stand in lines!"

With that John parted the sea of students, Fred following meekly in his wake. In a matter of moments, they had their food.

John smiled again as he saw Fred looking about for a place to sit. "Another privilege of teaching. We don't have to eat with the students. Follow me. I shall take you to the 'inner sanctum.'"

A loopy grin spread across Fred's face as they walked out of the cafeteria and into the hallway. "The teachers' lounge," Fred murmured. He blushed as he looked down at John. "It must seem silly to you, but well . . . the teachers' lounge!"

I could like this boy, John thought to himself, as he fought to keep from chuckling. "No, I understand. I remember the first time I sat in the teachers' lounge. It made me feel . . . I don't know, validated."

Fred nodded his head vigorously as they walked.

"Yeah, like I'm real."

"What an interesting way of putting it."

He had meant it as a compliment, but the boy blushed again and was silent. Before John could explain himself, Steve walked up and joined them.

"The clock is ticking, O great untall one. Are you an organ donor? Do you have a living will? Is there a next of kin? . . ."

John ignored him and looked up at his student teacher. "Don't mind him. He's challenged me to a pick-up game at four. He thinks that being tall is the only requirement for playing basketball." He then turned to Steve. "It's leverage son, leverage. Remember what that Greek said? 'Give me a place to stand and I will move the world!'"

"Greek? Your fraternity brothers won't help you at four o'clock."

"Boo. We'll see."

A light had gone on deep inside of Fred. "Basketball?" he asked reverently.

"You play?" both men asked in unison, both men sounding incredulous as they looked at the awkward young man before them.

"All the time."

They had arrived at the teachers' lounge, so they stopped and paused a moment. John cringed inwardly, knowing the next question had to be . . . "Would you like to join us at four o'clock?"

"Oh yes!" the boy said as he pumped his head enthusiastically.

Steve made eye contact with John as the three entered the lounge. John allowed the boy to pass in front of them, then shrugged his shoulders in a helpless gesture at his friend.

The gym was fairly busy at four o'clock. Varsity practice started at five o'clock, so many of the boys didn't bother to go home but hung around the gym. Of course, for every boy waiting to play there was at least one, sometimes two girls more than willing to wait with them.

When John had first started working out with Steve after school, he'd been a little shy with the many students sitting around the bleachers. He'd soon learned, though, that with all the intense flirting going on between the students, any adult was practically invisible.

He'd also learned to really look forward to his little pick-up games with Steve or any other semi-athletic teacher he could snag. John wasn't really aware of how small a social life he had. His world had shrunk severely over the years.

It was with some dread that he looked over at Fred. The boy was wearing a very baggy pair of sweats and a rather rumpled looking t-shirt. Fred didn't look like much of a player. It occurred to John that his student teacher must have had these clothes out in his car. In fact, the sweat pants had lighter streaks as if they'd been bleached by the sun, as if the pants spent most of their time in the car. John shook his head in amusement, hoping Fred wouldn't embarrass himself too badly.

John, of course, was dressed in a matching blue nylon running suit with spotlessly clean gym shoes. This was as casual as he could get. He was hopelessly fastidious when it came to his appearance. Not vain really, just extremely careful.

Steve walked up, talking a mile a minute. He dribbled a basketball in his right hand while he swung his coach's whistle in his left hand.

"Nice duds, John. Very elegant. Were you planning on just watching, then? Now Fred, he looks ready to play basketball, football or dig a ditch, even."

Fred blushed, not sure how to take Brooks's banter. It didn't matter, though, as Steve talked on.

"However, as you felt it necessary to enlist help, John, I too have engaged a second. I felt it would be rather tacky to beat both you and your apprentice single-hand-edly."

"It's all right, Fred. Our gym coach has a double-hinged jaw. He's a medical marvel that science is just now beginning to understand," John said calmly. He then quietly snatched the ball from Steve and made a neat basket from where he was standing. "Nothing but net . . . of course," John stated with the dignity of a benediction. "Now are we going to play or talk?"

"Play. Hey, David!" Steve yelled over John's head.

John winced not only from the volume but from the sound of the name. "David?" he grumbled soft enough for just Steve to hear.

"Oui, mon ami! Problem?" Steve asked pleasantly.

"He's not going to expect extra credit for this?"

Steve only smiled as David slowly left his girlfriend and other friends on the bleacher and ambled over. David was very popular within a certain group of students, a group of students that John had never cared for. They were all like David, spoiled and pampered, with parents who were forever sweeping in, demanding even more privileges for their little darlings.

David had a smirk on his face as he took in Fred's outfit. David was a walking advertisement of name-brand sports clothes. His tennis shoes alone had cost well over a hundred dollars. He obviously didn't think much of the new student teacher, though he took slightly more care in hiding his feelings about the other two teachers.

"Shirts and skins. I'll flip the coin, you call," Steve said as he dug into his pocket for a coin.

Fred scratched his head nervously and said, "Uh, maybe Mr. Allan and I could just go ahead and be shirts."

The memory of his wife's beliefs on Christian modesty came flooding back to John. He felt a wave of unwanted irritation wash over him as he snapped at Fred, "If it's that important to you."

Steve looked in amazement at John. He'd never heard him use that tone before with anyone. Mystified, he shrugged off his shirt and got ready to play. John felt bad immediately but he didn't explain or apologize.

Embarrassed and rattled, Fred was two left feet as they began to play. At one point, he even tripped and knocked into John, nearly sending them both to the floor. David laughed loudly and was joined by a chorus of hoots and catcalls from the bleachers.

His face a crimson red, Fred apologized to John. John shook his head.

"Don't worry about it, son," he said in his kindest tones, a direct contrast from his previous curt reply.

"Aren't we having the mood swings today, darling?" Steve whispered in John's ear.

John slammed the basketball into his stomach.

They hadn't played long before John saw that David Martin was a number one ball hog. He could make the shots, but it never occurred to him to pass off to Steve, his teammate. John noted with amusement how frustrated Steve was becoming with his star player.

Fred, on the other hand, seemed only too willing to pass off the ball. His earlier slip and Martin's laughter had trained every eye in the gym on their little game. He looked desperate, as if he only wanted this fiasco to be over.

David was eating it up. He was very aware of how good his form was and of how receptive an audience he had. He began to aggressively block the others' shots, even getting a few elbows into Fred.

John saw what was happening and called a time out. He raised his eyebrows meaningfully at Steve, then pulled Fred to one side.

"Fred, I'm really sorry about this. Usually, no one pays any attention to us. We certainly don't have audiences." Looking over at David, he added, "And we don't play with students like that. Anyway, Fred, if you'd like to quit now, I'd understand."

Fred became very serious as he answered, "Mr. Allan, I never quit anything."

Surprised, John nodded and signaled for the others to resume play. As they continued, Fred became more focused and intense. He didn't pass off the ball as much but started making some shots. Nothing tricky or flashy, but he and John began to rack up some points.

David's smirk had disappeared. He now found some of his own shots being blocked. The game was becoming very close. In the last moments of the game, David had lined up a beautiful shot, but just as the ball was leaving his hands, Fred reached in and slammed it to the floor. From there the ball bounced into John's waiting hands, who quickly won the game with the final basket.

For a moment everyone in the gym was silent. It had been too perfect. Then the catcalls and laughter began. Only now it was for David.

"Teachers!" someone yelled. "Dunkin' Dave was beaten by two teachers!"

"English teachers! He was beaten by English teachers!" another added.

"Whew, good thing the cafeteria ladies weren't here, huh Dave?"

That last little volley caused the most laughter. It came from his own girlfriend. David had totally lost his sense of humor. After staring hard at Fred, he stalked off to the shower room.

Steve smiled and gave both teachers a slap on the back. "Good game. I don't mind losing to you when my own teammate has such a . . ." he looked at Fred before he continued, "has such an attitude problem. He'll have to change some things if he's going to make it on varsity."

"Really, Steve, the boy just needs some encouragement. You should try it sometime," John replied in a singsong fashion.

"Get outta here. Besides, you know me, I'd sell my soul for one winning season," he laughed.

John winced, wondering if Fred would jump on Steve's lighthearted expression, but the young man only smiled politely.

"Well, this was fun. Thank you for letting me play. I guess I'll see you in the morning, Mr. Allan. I mean, I know I'll see you in the morning; there's no guessing, I mean." Fred faltered to a finish. "Uh, anyway, good night!" He gave a stilted little wave and walked out.

"You make him nervous . . . Mr. Allan, I mean," Steve joked gently.

John looked up sharply, surprised at such a direct statement. He took a moment to pull at a nonexistent wrinkle before he answered. "Me? You're the one who keeps making cracks about his clothes. 'Digging ditches' really!" He hurried on before Steve could comment, "Besides, the boy's just high strung. He's nervous with everyone."

"C'mon, John. This may be his first day, but your student teachers have usually elected you for sainthood by now. What gives?"

"I guess I'm just not a saint, all right?" he retorted with asperity.

"All right John, I'll cancel that letter to the pope. Besides . . . St. John, hm? I guess it's been done," Steve joked but his eyes were concerned.

John sighed deeply, glad to change the subject. "I'm sorry, Steve. I spend too much time with these moody teenagers. I seem to be having a hormonal imbalance of my own today."

"Well, if you start craving mass quantities of chocolate let me know; we'll go on a binge together."

"It's a deal. Are you and all the clan still coming over tonight?"

"The whole flying circus. Seven?"

"Seven."

A heavy load of guilt descended on John as he left the gym. Steve was right. He was making Fred nervous. He'd already snapped at him twice. He'd have to get a grip on himself. He didn't want to make Fred's student teaching experience any harder than necessary. John sighed when he thought of how hard that experience would be. Fred had just unknowingly alienated the leader of a very difficult group of students.

As John left the building he saw Fred standing with Clark Nelson in the parking lot. The two were certainly a study in contrasts. Clean-cut Fred in his old gym clothes was talking excitedly to Clark who was nodding his hacked and beaded hair up and down.

Instantly suspicious, John wondered if Fred had already begun his mission of converting the student body. John was very fond of Clark and didn't want him to have any part of Fred's religion. He decided to walk past and hear what they were talking about.

As he walked up he could hear the two were avidly discussing basketball. He noticed that Fred became ill at ease as he approached.

"Oh, hello, Mr. Allan."

"Hi, Mr. A," Clark said in his own slow fashion. "Looks like you got a pretty cool student teacher this time."

Fred managed to look embarrassed and happy at the same time. John realized it was probably the first positive thing to happen to the young man all day.

John tried to smile and nod in agreement, but his own conflicting emotions made him seem reserved. He saw that Fred noticed and looked away. Without wanting it, John could feel a gulf widening between him and his student teacher.

The next two weeks were two of the longest in John's memory. He had never been as uncomfortable around anyone as he was with Fred Evans. The boy himself couldn't have been nicer. It was what he represented that rubbed John raw.

John would be in the middle of a lesson, lost in the mechanics of a prepositional phrase, but one look at Fred watching from the back of the room could unlock a host of unwanted thoughts and feelings.

Did Fred really believe in this God of his? A God that let people, good Christian people, die?

Fred never tried to inject his beliefs into any conversation he had with John. In his own nervous way he would question him endlessly about presenting literature, about the finer points of phrases and clauses, but he would never mention God.

John knew how unfair he was being and it bothered him intensely. He knew that he wasn't preparing Fred enough, wasn't explaining enough, just plain wasn't spending enough time with the boy. But he could hardly bear to be around him. The anger and rage he thought he had buried with his poor wife had been resurrected. Fred as the touchstone was paying for all of it.

After Chris Williams had done such a creative job of butchering the classic *David Copperfield* during book reports, John had thought it would be a good thing to have his junior literature class read and study parts of the novel aloud. Incredibly, John had forgotten one very critical section of the novel.

On this particular afternoon Audrea Givens was reading aloud. A short, dark-haired girl, she had a nice clear reading voice, so John frequently called on her. He had allowed his mind to wander as he looked out over the classroom, making sure the others were reading along in their books. He could tell David Martin was using his book to cover up some magazine. John was just about to say something when Audrea's words broke through to him. She was reading the part where the hero's wife, Dora, dies.

John's eyes became chained to the page in front of him. How could he have forgotten? He was forced to sit quietly as the girl recounted the young woman's death. The character of Dora had always reminded him of his wife. Little and pretty, full of life, childlike, he had even told Linda of the similarity once. Also like his wife, the character had been expecting a child.

Several of his girl students were affected as Audrea read on. Most of his boy students were uncomfortable with the emotional scene and began to display exaggerated boredom. John was oblivious to it all. All the anger that he felt on the day of his wife's funeral reared up within him.

No one in the room knew very much about their teacher. Only a handful knew about his wife. It was hard for most students to picture Mr. Allan as having any sort of life outside of the classroom. As of late, he really didn't.

The room became quiet but John didn't notice. Audrea looked up, wondering if she should continue reading. Clark Nelson cleared his throat. "Why? Why did she die?"

John looked up sharply as he heard the very words that had echoed through his mind for fifteen years. It took him a moment to focus his eyes on the boy. "What did you say?" he demanded in his lowest tones.

Surprised at his teacher's reaction, Clark asked again. "Why did she die? What was the point?"

John stood up and thrust his hands into his pockets. "Why did she die? What was the point?" he repeated irritably. "Clark, how often I have asked myself those very questions." John turned to the back of the room. "Mr. Evans!" he called out sharply. "Perhaps you can explain to the class the point of this young woman dying."

Caught off guard, Fred rose unsteadily to his feet. "Well, sir, her character was vastly unsuited to the hero's and . . ."

"Unsuited?" John interrupted heatedly, "Unsuited? She was everything he ever wanted."

Fred's face went white at this challenge in front of the students. "True, sir, but she was not everything he needed, the author wanted . . ."

Again John interrupted the young man. "Not everything he needed?" he scoffed. "Oh, well then, let's sacrifice her by all means. She's dispensable, she's disposable. The author uses her for his ends then throws her away."

The students sat transfixed at this exchange. A few of the more astute realized Mr. Allan was not this passionate over a character in a book. John caught their stares and calmed himself. He walked over to the front of his desk and leaned against it. His fists were jammed in his pockets, his wedding ring biting into his hand.

"Perhaps Mr. Evans subscribes to the Victorian view of the novel. All things are to be endured and suffered at the hands of the all-knowing God. You see, class, the Victorians . . ."

The bell cut him off in midsentence. He gave a nod towards the door, dismissing the class. The students filed out silently, subdued by their favorite teacher's thinly veiled anger.

Fred Evans still stood in the back of the room, confused and uncertain. John waited until every student was gone before he looked at him.

"Mr. Evans."

"Yes, sir?"

"Since you seem to have such a firm grasp of this novel, I'll be turning this class over to you as of tomorrow."

"Tomorrow?" Fred said weakly.

"Yes, I'm sure you can handle it. Now if you'll excuse me." John turned on his heel and left, leaving a very shaken young man alone in his classroom.

John walked down to the lounge, glad this class was the last of the day. Thankfully, he saw that he was the only one in the lounge. He sat down on the couch and tried to think.

What am I doing? he thought as he stared at the ceiling. How can I be acting like this? Fred's not ready to teach a class. And he's certainly not ready to teach that class. Not my eleventh graders; they'll crucify him.

The opening of the lounge door interrupted his thoughts. John looked over to see Renee Grayson smiling at him. Of course, he thought, of course it had to be her.

"John, dear!" she gushed. "How are you? It seems simply ages since we've spoken."

She ignored all the empty chairs in the room and sat beside him on the couch. John doubted a slip of paper would have fit between them.

Today her hair was artistically wrapped with a black scarf. She wore a silky, long, black shirt over black leggings. John supposed she looked attractive, but all he could think of was a black cat with very long claws. Claws that she wanted to sink into him.

"I haven't forgotten that dinner I owe you," she smiled big, "and I pay off all my debts."

John smiled uncertainly, hoping she wouldn't invite him tonight. He knew his brain was too tired to come up with any plausible excuses.

"How about . . ."

But the door, opening again, saved him.

"Steve!" he called out gratefully, "There you are! I've been looking all over for you."

Steve just stood in the doorway, a lopsided grin on his face, taking in the little tableau before him. "I can't imagine why."

"Well . . . I was wondering if you'd heard any more about the possibilities of a strike."

The smile left Steve's face. He shook his head and sat down opposite the couch. "Only what you already know. The levy goes up for a vote on Friday night. If it doesn't pass, the union strikes."

"I hear one of the school board members, Marvin Wilkerson, is even campaigning against the levy," Renee commented bitterly. "He's got most of the senior citizens against it already."

Steve shrugged. "The senior citizens are on fixed incomes and Wilkerson owns a lot of real estate. Neither is going to welcome new property taxes."

"Gee, Steve, are you sure you know whose side you're on?" Renee's laughter was laced with irritation. She would have been a lot more direct if John hadn't been in the room. She had never liked Steve Brooks and she only bothered to hide it when John was around.

She stood and made an elaborate stretch. "Well, boys, I have to go help some students practice for our next play." She looked meaningfully at John, "We'll talk later."

John waited until the door closed behind her before he spoke again. His hazel eyes danced as he spoke. "Thank you, thank you, thank you."

"Can you translate that gratitude into a ride home? My better half took the car today."

John stood and waved towards the door. "Master, your carriage awaits."

As the two men walked down the hall, John saw that the light was still on in his room. He purposely looked away, not wanting to know if Fred was in there. It's just as well that he did, or he would have seen Fred seated at his desk, his head bowed in prayer.

8

All the next morning John worried about Fred teaching his junior literature class. He would look up from his desk to see Fred writing away in a lesson plan book. Before long Fred had run out of room and was writing on notebook paper. At least, John thought, the boy is going to be well prepared. He hoped.

At noon, as the students filed out, John asked Fred if he wouldn't like to stop and get something to eat. Fred looked up from the mound of papers in his lap and shook his head. "No, no, thank you. I'd like to stay in the room and, uh, practice."

"Practice?"

As usual, Fred blushed to the roots of his hair. "Well, yes. I wanted to be sure I stand correctly. I thought I'd work on the board some, so I thought I'd practice writing first."

"Oh."

"Yes, they say a lot of students are visual learners, so I thought I could reinforce that by providing visual stimulus on the board while they receive the auditory input through the reading—"

"Fred?" John interrupted gently.

"Yes, sir?"

"Don't turn your back on them . . . ever."

"Yes, sir," Fred answered meekly, a new look of fear coming into his eyes.

John stood and looked uncertainly at the young man before him. He really regretted his haste yesterday. This boy wasn't ready for his eleventh graders. He should have started him with some eager-to-please ninth graders, or even his know-it-all seniors.

"Well, then, I'll be going to lunch."

As John walked through the halls he kept thinking of the Roman emperor Nero. He wondered how that man had felt when he had sent Christians to their death with the lions. He doubted Nero had ever felt as guilty as he was feeling now.

The two classes right after lunch seemed to sail by despite the frequent clock watching by both John and his student teacher. All too soon it was the last class of the day.

As the students came in John studied every boy and most of the girls. Were they carrying any concealed weapons? Would an assault rifle fit into a gym bag? he asked himself.

When the last student was seated, John rose and addressed the class.

"As you all know, Mr. Evans is working hard towards becoming a teacher. With this goal in mind I felt it would be appropriate for him to lead the class in our current study of *David Copperfield*." Several students shifted in their seats to exchange a knowing look with their friends. John saw it but continued, "I trust you will afford him the same courtesy you always give me." John made a small motion towards his desk. "Mr. Evans."

Fred walked towards the front of the room, his planning book bursting with papers. A pile of books that had been under David Martin's desk suddenly appeared in the aisle. Fred's foot became entangled and he lurched forward, his papers going everywhere. The class burst into laughter.

John silenced them with a glance. "David, pick up those papers for Mr. Evans please."

David started to protest, but the look on his teacher's face got through even to him. After a few moments Fred was organized enough to take his seat at the desk and begin the day's lesson. Feeling he might never see the young man again, but knowing Fred could never teach with him in the room, John nodded and left.

Fred felt a brief moment of relief when the door closed behind his supervising teacher, a brief moment that evaporated as soon as he turned to see the sea of faces before him. Many of the students had assumed a sullen expression solely for the purpose of rattling him. It worked.

"Yes, well, I thought because there are so many characters and story lines in the book it might be helpful to put them up on the board."

As Fred stood he looked down at his careful lesson plans on the desk, lesson plans that were now hopelessly out of order. He felt a wave of panic wash over him.

He turned to the blackboard and began to write, forgetting Mr. Allan's warning about never turning his back on the class. Almost immediately there was a sharp metallic crack as something hit the board beside his head.

He whipped around to look at the class, only to see the same mass of sullen faces. Unsure of what to do, he decided to ignore it.

"You see, class, there are several stories within this one novel." Fred felt every drop of moisture leave his mouth as he continued to talk. "First, we have the story of David and his mother and Peggoty."

Fred tried to write these names on the board while he faced the class but he couldn't manage it without turning his head. The moment he did he was rewarded with two metallic pings close to his ear.

He stopped and tried to look sternly at the class, but the hateful expressions on most of their faces dried up anything he could do.

"Now, just what is that noise?"

No one spoke. A few students, like Audrea Givens and Clark Nelson, looked sympathetic but the student's code of silence bound them.

Fred forged on with the remainder of the lesson but his dry mouth made it nearly impossible to speak and he knew the moment he turned his head or looked down he'd hear that mysterious metallic ping on the board.

By two-thirty Fred was sure that the only sound more welcome than the dismissal bell would be the blowing of Gabriel's trumpet. In his nervousness he had rushed through his lesson and now faced another half hour totally unprepared. So it was with the greatest gratitude that he saw David Martin's raised hand.

"Yes, David?"

"I don't understand what you have on the board there. How was Steerforth related to Mr. Peggoty?"

As Fred turned to the board to explain he found himself in a perfect shower of thrown pennies. The loud metallic crash they made on the board reverberated through the room. As he whipped back to face the class he was met with the same wall of stony faces he had seen all period.

Meanwhile, John Allen was staring at the clock in the teacher's lounge. An untasted cup of coffee was in his hands as he sat in the chair opposite the clock.

He was alone with a cartload of guilt and regret. He had hated prejudice all his life, yet here he was playing the part of a bigot. A religious bigot. Sure, he could rant about separation between church and state, but Fred had never tried to cross those lines.

No, he told himself, you're cheating Fred of a decent internship because of his religious beliefs. Beliefs he hasn't even tried to share with you. He couldn't (or at least he shouldn't) fault Fred for loving the same God his wife had. Oh, Linda, you wouldn't be very happy with me right now.

John suddenly sat up straight in his chair. Even in his innermost thoughts, he had never addressed his wife in the present tense. Where had that come from? What if? What if she did exist on some other plane? Even with God? He shook his head at that, convinced he was letting his imagination get carried away. The sound of approaching footsteps made him look up.

"John?" It was Sarah Dunlap, the chemistry teacher. She was a tall, attractive redhead. Her green eyes expressed concern as she looked down at him. "John, what are you doing here at two-thirty? Are you all right?"

He leaned back in his chair and sighed.

"Oh, I was just channeling," he said ruefully. "You know, having an out-of-body experience, trying to reach a higher cosmic plane."

"Well, you'd better get body and soul together. I just heard an awful commotion coming from your room. I think they're trying to lynch your student teacher."

9

"You know, I think we have enough money here to buy a couple of sodas. If only the machine would take pennies," John said with gentle humor.

Fred looked up from the desk, a look of infinite sadness on his face. "I'm really sorry, Mr. Allan," his voice echoed in the empty classroom. "You told me not to turn my back on them."

John only shrugged. He took the broom he was holding and finished sweeping up the coins into a dusty mound. He then knelt and took a piece of cardboard and scooped the money into a paper bag. As he stood, he turned and smiled at Fred. "I think I'll have David Martin wash each of these individually."

"But I can't be sure he threw any," Fred replied.

"I can."

John set the bag down and pulled out a handkerchief to wipe his hands. He then sat down in a chair across from the young man. Twenty years of teaching left him unfazed at today's little episode. He knew there were far worse things to be thrown than pennies. He was glad Fred was student teaching at a school in a small rural town like Glendale. He'd known of big city teachers who'd had to

71

place metal screens around their desks for protection. No, at Glendale you wouldn't look up to see a brick coming at you. At least not so far.

He looked up at the blackboard behind Fred. "You had a good idea, you know."

"Really?" Fred asked in surprise.

"Sure. It was just the wrong class. You can do things with some classes that you'd never dream of doing with others. Take the freshman literature class for instance. Those kids love order and structure. They would have copied your story lines down without a peep."

"Really?"

"Really. Fred, what happened today happens in some form to all teachers. As my supervising teacher told me, 'You just get back on that horse and ride.'"

"Thank you," the boy answered, sounding very unconvinced. He looked down at the desk and continued in a small, quiet voice, "Thank you, but . . . I've felt, I know, you haven't been very happy with me."

John was struck to the heart. He shook his head. "No, son, that's not true."

Fred looked up. He was polite, but he spoke with sad confidence. "I think we both know that it is."

John was silent. He knew the young man deserved an explanation for his often aloof and moody behavior. But his inner pain wasn't something he had ever shared. How could he tell it to this mere boy? What if he started preaching at him or gave him some empty platitudes? John didn't think he could stand it.

Fred took his silence as an affirmation of his worst fears. "If you want another student teacher, I'll understand."

"Oh, no, Fred! Listen, I need to tell you a few things . . ."

John was prevented from continuing by the sound of loud voices coming down the hallway towards his room. They both looked up to see Brooks and Calvin Loring coming in the door. They were arguing as usual.

"It's an outrage, Steve! It just shows you what they think of us in this town!"

"Calvin, you take everything so personal. I'm sure they were only thinking of the tax write-off. It wasn't a statement of your worth as a teacher."

"Wasn't it? Let's get John's opinion, since you have so little faith in mine."

Loring loomed over John. His white dress shirt had sweat stains even on this mild day. He was carrying a battered cardboard box in his beefy arms. He threw it down in disgust on the desk, then turned to John. "Do you remember the local business that promised to donate twenty computers to the school?"

John had a whimsical temptation to ask if they were in the box, but another look at Loring's glowering face stopped him.

"Yes," he answered tentatively.

"Well, just look at this!" Loring reached into the box and pulled out some of the largest computer disks John had ever seen. They looked to be nearly ten inches across.

"Good heavens," he said as he took one from Loring and examined it. "I've never seen anything like this."

Loring crossed his arms over his barrel chest and nodded his head. "There's a reason for that. They come from computers that have been out-of-date for years. They had the gall to unload twenty useless dinosaurs on me. The only thing my students can do on these pieces of trash is play with the power buttons and type their names!"

"I can see why you'd be disappointed."

"Disappointed? I'm furious. I tell you, Allan, it's a message. That business is telling us what they think of us. They're laughing at this school."

"Well, I wouldn't go that far . . ." Steve started.

"Wouldn't you? Let me tell you, you'll change your mind when that levy fails to pass. Then what are you going to say about these things?" Loring waved a fist full of disks at him.

"They'll make nice signs for the picket line?" Steve quipped.

Loring threw the disks back into the box. He picked the box up in a huff and went to the door. He turned back in the doorway. "You're a riot, Brooks," he said angrily. "I just hope you only hear the word 'scab' in your First Aid class."

"Hey!" Steve exclaimed, stung. "That's uncalled for!"

"Is it? You've never been supportive of the union. Not at all. You'll fall off that fence you've been riding if that levy doesn't pass and a strike is called. I'll just be curious to see on whose side you land."

After Loring left, Steve paced up and down in front of the room in agitation. John walked up and tried to place a calming hand on his arm. But his friend shook it off. "Thanks for standing up for me, John."

"Steve!"

"Yeah? Well, you were pretty quiet there when Loring was letting me have it. I thought maybe you agreed with him."

"Not at all."

Steve stopped pacing and ran a shaky hand through his hair. He let out a deep breath. "I don't do anger very well," he looked over at Fred. "We put on quite a show for you, son. Sure you still want to be a teacher?"

Fred just nodded, his blue eyes huge.

"Well, gentlemen, until tomorrow." Steve tried to regain his usual tone but failed.

"I'll call you later, Steve," John said as he walked with him to the hallway.

Steve gave him an unreadable look and nodded before he walked away.

John's thoughts were troubled as he walked back into the room. Steve was the only real friend he had. Why hadn't he jumped down Loring's throat? Then here was

Fred, a boy he'd undermined from day one. What was the matter with him? When had he become so self-centered?

Fred was still sitting at the desk, toying with one of the huge computer disks.

"I imagine you've never seen anything like that before, have you, Fred?" John asked kindly, hoping for a neutral topic.

"Actually, I have. Mom has some of these lying around the house. My dad used to work with computers." He looked closer at the sleeve label and smiled. "In fact, he worked for this very company."

John smiled too. "Now that's a coincidence. You'll have to tell your dad about all this when you get home."

Fred made a small shrugging motion with his shoulders. "My father's deceased."

"I'm sorry to hear that."

He shrugged again. "It's been a long time. I'm afraid I don't remember him very well. I was only five when he died, and he'd been so sick a good year before that." He looked up from the disk and said simply, "Cancer."

John's attention was riveted to the nervous young man before him. Had his dad been a Christian like Fred? Like Linda? What did he think of his father dying like that? How did he explain it?

Of course a father's death couldn't be as devastating as a wife's or husband's could it? John tried to hide his curiosity as only polite concern.

"I'm sure it must have been very hard for your mother."

"Yes, I'm sure it was."

Fred had a peace as he spoke that John couldn't understand. John longed to question him more closely, but he knew that it would be out of the bounds of good manners. He hesitated, wanting to ask if Fred or his family had known his wife. He stopped himself though. He didn't want a carload on his doorstep every night begging him to come to church.

"Well, anyway, I want you to know I think you'll be fine here. Just take back the class tomorrow, like nothing ever happened."

Fred nodded gratefully.

John nodded back and walked to the door. "I'm glad you're here, Fred. I wouldn't want another student teacher," he lied through his teeth.

That night when he called Steve's house his wife answered. She told him that Steve wasn't home. John wished she hadn't sounded so strange when she said it.

The next day when John turned the junior class over to him, Fred decided to try nothing more creative than having the class read aloud. Things went pretty smoothly at first, although Fred was troubled by the constant bad smell. He couldn't figure out where it was coming from or what it was.

About five minutes into class David Martin approached the desk. He spoke quietly as another student was still reading aloud.

"Mr. Evans, I gotta go!" he whispered urgently.

"Go where?" Fred asked with concern.

"Aw, you know. The bathroom!"

"Oh, yes, you may go."

David looked vastly uncomfortable as he whined, "The hall pass. I gotta have the hall pass!"

"Oh, yes, of course." Fred fished around the pile of papers on the desk looking for something that might be a hall pass.

"Pleeeze, Mr. Evans! I'm desperate."

As David had raised his voice, a few titters of laughter came from the class. Hating the disruption, Fred began pulling open drawers in his search.

"Mr. Evans!" David urged louder, causing the reader to stop and Fred to look even harder.

David pulled a folded piece of paper from his pocket. He danced from foot to foot, causing uproarious laughter from the class. "Here, can ya just sign this?"

"Yes, yes, just go!" the very flustered student teacher said as he scrawled his name on the paper. David ran from the room, slamming the door behind him.

"David! That's uncalled for!" But his words were lost in the loud merriment of the class.

It was a good five minutes before Fred could restore any sort of order to the class. Finally though, he was able to calm them down enough to start the reading again. Ten minutes dragged by. All the while Fred was trying to figure out where the awful smell was coming from. He opened a few windows, but it didn't help very much.

One of the students, Jackie Chambers, raised her hand. "Mr. Evans! It's three o'clock."

Several students rose from their desks when she said this.

"What? Wait a minute everyone . . ." Fred said in surprise as he looked at the clock. "Well, I guess . . . but why hasn't the bell rung?"

"Oh, it does that sometimes."

"Yeah, it breaks down a lot."

"Happens all the time!"

The whole class began to agree it was nearly a daily event.

"Okay, class dismissed," he said with relief.

The students were out the door in a rush. Fred leaned back in his chair and savored the quiet. He offered up a prayer of thanks for having gotten through the class with so little trouble. He just wished that awful smell would go away. Then it occured to him that some of the students came from bad circumstances; maybe they didn't know the finer points of personal hygiene.

A few minutes ticked by with Fred wondering why Mr. Allan didn't come back. He also began to notice how very quiet it was. Much too quiet for the end of the day rush. Curious and wanting to get away from the foul-smelling classroom, Fred picked up his briefcase from beside the desk and walked out into the hallway.

Funny, he thought, that smell is out here too. He also noticed with rising dismay that the other classrooms were full of students. Fred's heart sank as he saw Mr. Allan and Jim Gilman, the principal, coming at a good speed from the far end of the hallway. There was a look of profound annoyance on both their faces. Mr. Allan was smoothing his lapels down, a gesture Fred had already learned meant he was agitated.

John walked up to him, his hazel eyes bright and angry. "Mr. Evans," he said in a voice of low thunder, "we really must talk." He made a curt motion back towards the classroom.

He waited until Fred and the principal passed before him and then followed them into the room. He shut the door with a decided click, his maturity being the only factor keeping him from slamming it.

John's nose twitched. What in the world was that smell? He wondered for a moment but dismissed it as irrelevent.

"Mr. Evans, with authority comes a great responsibility. We are morally and legally responsible for these children until three o'clock every day.

"To me, the legal responsibility comes a distant second to the moral obligation for their welfare . . ."

"That legal responsibility is pretty important too!" Mr. Gilman interrupted, his gray eyes blazing through his glasses. "Think of the lawsuits if one of those kids were hurt . . ."

"We could be the indirect cause of profound consequences . . ." John began.

"Consequences? Think of the parents! Man, you wouldn't believe some of the ringers we have in that class. Their folks would haul us into court so fast your head would spin!"

Fred's head was spinning pretty good already. He had absolutely no idea what they were talking about. Though he stood a good ten inches over both men, at the moment he felt very, very small.

Jim Gilman was roughly the same size as John Allan. But there all similarity ended. His gray hair was thick and curly and he wore it as far down on his collar as a principal could get away with. A good and caring man, he possessed a temper that was nothing short of legendary. His temper had the quality of a force of nature. There was nothing to be done about it; one just hoped there were survivors when it was over.

He was nearly shaking now, he was so angry. His face was beet red and his eyes were almost squinted shut behind his glasses. His teeth showed white and fierce under his moustache. Absurdly, Fred was reminded of a caricature he'd seen of President Teddy Roosevelt.

Mr. Gilman pulled a white sheet of paper from his suit and thrust it under Fred's nose.

"Would you like to explain this, young man?"

Fred took the paper and read the following words:

Dear Mr. Gilman:

I have better things to do this afternoon than teach this stupid book. I'm letting the class leave early.

Sincerely,
Mr. Evans

10

"**I**, I never wrote that!" Fred spluttered.

John's face cleared immediately, but the principal looked unconvinced. "I've got your signature on several papers in the office, son! Tell me you didn't write that," Mr. Gilman said skeptically.

"Wait. David Martin did give me a piece of paper to sign as a hall pass." Fred turned the folded sheet over in his hand. "You know I think I did sign this, but really, I never wrote the rest!"

"David Martin, huh? Well that explains the note, but why on earth did you let those kids out at two-thirty in the afternoon?"

Fred was the very picture of misery as he silently mouthed the word "two-thirty." "The clock said it was three, so I dismissed them. Honestly."

In unison the two older men turned to look at the clock. They then looked at their watches. The mystery was solved. Mr. Gilman made eye contact with John and muttered, "Green as grass."

Gilman shook his head and looked wearily up at Fred. He took the paper back from the boy.

"I'll take care of David Martin. John, you take care of him."

Mr. Gilman was nearly to the door, then he turned and looked with disgust at John. "Phew! Smell that? I'll bet the pipes are backed up again." He looked suspiciously at Fred as if he just might be responsible, then turned and left.

Fred stood in the middle of the room, looking as if a high wind had passed over him. John sat down at his desk, torn between being amused or annoyed. "I should have known you'd never write a note like that. I'm sorry, Fred. By the way, why did you sign a piece of paper for David?"

"He needed a hall pass for the bathroom."

John reached to the side of his desk where a small wooden block was hanging on a hook. He held it up. "Hall Pass" was printed neatly on its side.

"Oh," Fred said bleakly.

John shook his head and smiled. He rose from his chair and walked to the back of the room. He took the clock down from the wall and reset it to the proper time. He replaced it and looked back at Fred. "It's an old trick. I wonder when they changed the time on it." John stopped and took a sideways glance at the unhappy young man. "You turned your back again, didn't you?" he chided gently.

"Well, yes, just once. I opened the windows. I wanted to get that awful smell out of here."

"What is that anyway? I've never smelt anything—" John was interrupted by the sight of Sarah Dunlap in the doorway. She was wearing an irritated expression that turned to revulsion when she walked into the room.

"Oh, dear! I'm afraid it's too late."

"What's too late, Sarah?"

"I had a big bucket of dead frogs that I was getting ready to treat with formaldehyde. You know, so the kids could start dissecting next week."

"Yes?" John had an awful feeling he knew where this was heading.

"Well, the bucket's been missing since this morning. I was hoping to find the frogs before they started to rot." She sniffed the air. "It may be too late, but I think I found them."

She took a few tentative steps towards Fred, sniffing all the while. He was amazed when she stopped in front of him. She looked down towards the briefcase he was carrying.

"So . . . when was the last time you opened your briefcase, Fred?"

"Lunchtime, why?"

"Allow me." She gently took the briefcase from him and gave it a little shake. It made a strange, wet, squishy sound. The smell seemed to get worse.

"No! Oh, no! Not my briefcase!"

Fred looked sorrowfully at his briefcase. Sarah placed her hand over her mouth for a moment then shook her head and looked at John.

"The eleventh grade?" she asked.

"The eleventh grade." He nodded. "Do you have anything important in there, Fred? I mean, do we really need to open it?"

"Well, yes, I have my . . ." he sniffed again as he took the case back from Sarah. "No, nothing that could be saved," he said mournfully.

"All right, let's open the rest of these windows. Then I'll walk you to the dumpster." John turned to the science teacher. "Sorry about the frogs, Sarah."

"Sorry about the briefcase. I guess we'll round up the usual suspects in the morning, John." She nodded at both of them and walked out.

John looked up at Fred. "You've had quite a week. Let's go give that briefcase a proper burial." The two left the classroom and went down the hall towards the stairs.

"You know the last time Sarah had frogs for dissecting, we found them all over the school for the next week.

Everytime I'd bend over to take a drink from the water fountain a little frog leg would be waving at me from the spigot," John commented.

Fred just smiled weakly.

"I must say, you have a really good attitude about this. I don't think I could have taken it so well if they'd ruined my briefcase."

"They never would have done it to your briefcase."

John smiled sheepishly and rubbed the back of his neck. It was true. The kids had a very healthy respect for him that bordered a little on fear.

"Just don't ever take it personally, Fred. Teenagers will do in a group what they would never consider doing individually. There were probably a few today that were very much against what happened."

"Why didn't they say so? I mean, the whole class left the room."

John sighed and looked up at Fred. "Oh, Fred, you're still a young man. Surely, you remember your high school years. You remember how peer pressure can force you to go along with the crowd, make you do what you know is wrong."

Fred was quiet for a moment, then in a very serious voice he said, "Actually, I always tried to do what was right. But it did get a little lonely at times."

There was an honesty in Fred's tone that spoke volumes to John. This wasn't sanctimonious bragging. He was just stating a fact. It occurred to John that he really hadn't tried to look at things from this young man's point of view. True, the boy was nervous and highstrung, but John was beginning to suspect there was solid steel in his backbone.

As they walked down the stairs John wondered what college life must be like for Fred. He couldn't imagine him being very comfortable with a lot of the social life there. Perhaps he had a lot of friends from his church. John found himself hoping that he did.

When they arrived at the first floor they turned left down the hallway. As they stopped in front of the office, John pointed to the nearest exit. "The dumpster is through there, son. Why don't you get rid of that thing while I go in and check my mail?" John took a deep breath and finished with, "There are still some things I'd like to talk to you about." He'd made up his mind to explain a little about his wife. Not too much, just enough to clear the way for a decent working relationship with the boy.

Fred was instantly uncomfortable. Now what? He wondered as he went out the door. John had to chuckle to himself. The boy was an open book. He could read his every thought. Shaking his head, John went into the office.

The school office was really four large rooms. The first room was for the school's two secretaries and accessible to anyone. To the left, was the office of the viceprincipal, Mr. Schwendeman. He was in charge of discipline, so only troublemakers went there. To the right was the teacher's mailroom, just for the teachers. Directly behind the secretaries' room was the principal's office, where hardly anyone went.

Mr. Gilman didn't have time for a lot of interaction. In fact his coming all the way up to John's third floor classroom had been a very rare event. He was strictly a behind-the-scenes administrator, trying to wrestle with the daily challenges of a small budget. John smiled to himself as he thought of the yearly "Gilman sighting" event the teachers had every fall. The first teacher to spot Mr. Gilman out of his office in the middle of a school day won fifty dollars. John hadn't won it yet.

As John made his way to the mailroom he was rather surprised to see a very large manila envelope in his mail chute. Picking it up he was surprised to see it was addressed in pencil to Fred.

Oh no, he thought to himself, someone's learned how

85

to make a mail bomb. He picked it up gingerly. There wasn't any ticking. As he carefully felt the package, it seemed to hold just a book and some papers. Should I open it? Should I give this to that poor boy? John asked himself.

John looked up to see Fred standing in the doorway. He shrugged and held the envelope out to Fred. "It's for you . . . be careful."

Fred was as leery as John. He felt the package for a few moments, but then a smile broke out on his face. He tore open the envelope and pulled out his old battered Bible.

"Look! It's here! Praise God, Mr. Allan. I thought I'd lost my dad's Bible to those stupid frogs!" He carefully laid the Bible on the counter and began pulling out various papers from the envelope. "Look at this! It's everything I had in my briefcase." He shoved the papers back into the envelope and picked up the Bible lovingly from the counter. It wasn't much to look at. Its spine had been broken, and a large thick rubber band was holding its frayed cover to the ragged sheets within.

"Yeah! Wow, I thought it was gone for good!" Fred was grinning from ear to ear. "Wow, it's okay now. I mean, at least one of those kids knows how to do what's right. Isn't this great, Mr. Allan?"

John found that he was grinning too, caught up by the boy's enthusiasm. He never would have dreamed he'd been so glad to see a Bible.

"Yes, Fred. It is great." He was suddenly reminded of his wife's Bible. Linda had had a real affection for her Bible too. He sobered for a moment, thinking of her.

"This was really nice of someone. They could have let it get ruined. Wow, maybe it was more than one, maybe it was a couple of kids. They're not so bad, are they Mr. Allan? The class just got carried away, huh?"

"Mmm? Yes, that's right." John gently took the Bible from the young man. The words "Holy Bible" could barely be traced in their golden ink. "This must be pretty old," he commented absently.

"Yes, sir. Mom gave it to Dad in 1970. She said he had it with him all the time. She said he had it with him when he died."

John went cold inside. He promptly handed the Bible back to Fred as he looked up at him with bitter eyes. He was silent for a moment, then he decided to speak. With the greatest restraint possible, he said, "I can relate, Fred. My wife had her Bible right beside her when she died too." He held back for a moment longer, then said what he really had wanted to say all along, "And it didn't make one little bit of difference, did it? Not one bit."

"Mr. Allan . . ."

John raised his hand for silence, then looked about the mailroom to make sure they were alone. He took a moment to smooth down his lapels and to straighten his cuffs before he could trust himself to speak again. "Fred, I don't plan on getting into some religious debate with you. But I know I've been . . . moody . . . and less than fair with you. I'm sorry. I'm sorry for a lot of things that have nothing to do with you. I've let some old memories cloud my professionalism." He paused not sure how to express himself. "Look, Fred, my wife believed in everything you do, in the same way that you do. It didn't make any difference at all. She died just the same." John stopped and smoothed down his little fringe of hair. "I'm sorry, I don't mean to disillusion you."

"You haven't."

John pulled at the pocket flaps on his suit, afraid he had said too much. "That's good, Fred. Enough said then. I just thought I owed you some sort of explanation."

"Mr. Allan . . ."

John held his hand up again. He had a sad little smile on his face as he shook his head. "So . . . did you know the eleventh grade has book reports due tomorrow?" he asked briskly.

"Yes, sir."

"Good. Now let me warn you . . ." John talked on as he led Fred out into the hallway and towards the main exit.

Fred had to smile at the unusual flow of words coming from his normally quiet instructor. He silently thanked God for the insight he had just been given into this man's soul. For the first time, Fred felt relaxed in the man's presence.

As they left the building they entered the parking lot. There were plenty of students there, but they couldn't help but notice Audrea Givens and Clark Nelson. They were staring fixedly at the far corner of the lot. They both had their backs to Fred and John so they didn't hear them approach. As they walked up to the two students it sounded like they were counting.

"Ten, nine, eight . . ." they chanted in unison.

"Audrea, Clark?" John intoned curiously.

Audrea whipped around with a guilty expression on her face, but Clark was not so easily rattled.

"'Lo, Mr. A, 'lo Mr. Evans, how's it goin'?" he asked calmly. He turned to face them, still keeping an eye on the far corner of the lot. Today, he was wearing feathered clips in his braided hair. They moved gently in the afternoon breeze.

Suddenly two loud yells were heard from the corner lot. The high and low tones identified them as a girl and a boy. The yells were immediately followed by the loud slamming of car doors.

Everyone in the parking lot turned to see David Martin and his girlfriend jumping up and down beside his car. The distance prevented John's group from hearing everything they were yelling, but a few choice words drifted back.

"My car! The upholstery!"

"My hair! They're in my hair!"

As the girl was becoming hysterical, several female

students raced to her aide. But the boys closest to David and his car were finding something very funny.

Fred looked uncertainly at John. "Shouldn't we go see what's wrong, Mr. Allan?"

"You've had a long day, Mr. Evans. I'll handle this. See you in the morning."

John smiled until the puzzled Fred got into his car and drove away. He then looked out of the corner of his eye at Audrea and Clark. He put a fatherly hand on Clark's shoulder.

"Clark, Clark, Clark," he said in a singsong fashion. "Just what do you suppose could be wrong with David's brand-new sports car?"

"Beats me."

"That's a thought, but I don't think it would help."

"Well, Mr. A, if I've told Dave once I've told him a hundred times not to leave his windows down. He's kinda careless that way."

"This time of year things could fly in."

"Or hop," Audrea added helpfully.

"Or hop," Clark agreed. "Then once things got in there, maybe they couldn't get out again." Clark lazily hooked his thumbs in the belt hooks of his low-slung pants. He slowly nodded his feathered head. "Yep, imagine if they died in there."

John just stood there, savoring the moment.

11

The next morning heads rolled. As John had suspected, David Martin had been the mastermind of the forged note and the class leaving early. John was also sure he was responsible for the frogs in Fred's briefcase, but that was a little harder to prove.

At any rate, David had certainly paid a high price. Starting tomorrow he would serve a three-day school suspension. Normally, that wouldn't faze a boy like David, but tomorrow was Friday, when Glendale would play its first basketball game of the season. The school was slated to play against Central, their biggest rival. David had worked like a dog in class and in the gym in order to be eligible for the team. Steve had promised he would be the starting center at tomorrow's game. That was all impossible now. So David had been on a slow burn all day.

John didn't feel sorry in the least for David, but he did feel bad for Steve. He tried to tell him that during lunch in the teacher's lounge. Steve was sitting in a corner of the lounge, far away from everyone else.

"Steve," John said, as he pulled up a chair beside him. "I'm really sorry that David can't play for you tomorrow."

"Yeah? I bet you're not half as sorry as I am," he said sourly as he continued to look down at a magazine.

"I don't see that I had any choice. You do know what he did?"

Steve looked up from his magazine, his face a blank. "One stinking day. His suspension just couldn't wait until Monday, could it?"

"What? You do know what he did?" John asked again, amazed at Steve's attitude.

"You've never liked that boy."

"What?"

"I understand the whole class walked out on that student teacher of yours, but David is the only one to get suspended. And of course his suspension has to start on the first day of the basketball season."

"I can't believe . . ."

"Believe whatever you want, John. Tomorrow we would have had a real chance at Central, but you fixed that." Steve made a move to get up, but John laid a restraining hand on his arm.

As several people were looking their way, he tried to lower his voice. "Look, Steve, this isn't like you. You've never cared that much about the games before. You're a first-class educator, not just a coach. What is all this?"

Steve twisted the magazine in his hands for a few moments before he answered. He didn't look up. When he spoke it was barely a whisper. "You know they vote on the levy tomorrow." He shook his head. "It won't pass. You also know the strike will be called when it doesn't pass." The big man let out a long sigh. "Tomorrow night my team had a first-class chance at winning. That would have meant everyone would have been pretty happy with this old coach. I wanted that." He looked up at John with sad and weary eyes. "Because, John, after that strike is called no one around here is ever going to be happy with me again."

John looked across the room and saw Calvin Loring

pretending not to pay any attention to them. John shook his head as he thought of what lay in store for his friend. He patted Steve on the arm. "You're sure then?" he whispered. "You're sure you want to cross the picket line?"

Steve's own guilt made him misinterpret John's concern as an accusation. "You don't have a family to be concerned about. I do!" he retorted without thinking.

Something shut down deep within John. He stood up and gave a little tug to his jacket. "I know I don't have a family," he said in low frigid tones. "I'm aware of it every day of my life."

Steve could only look miserably after him as John walked out the door, his back stiff and forbidding.

The next two periods, John was strictly on automatic. He listened to book reports without really comprehending, his face set in a somber expression. The classes were subdued by his mood.

He sat rigidly at his desk with his hands folded in front of him. His clear hazel eyes were half-lidded as he watched the students. Many of them were about fifteen, the age his child would have been. As he looked out over the classroom he wondered what his child would have been like.

He'd always loved children. Always. But to have one of your very own. To share your life with one. All the students in the world couldn't fill that gap.

As the book reports droned on, he wondered if he'd have had a boy. A son that he could have played basketball with. Or what about a girl? John nearly smiled, thinking of how she'd have had him wrapped around her little finger.

John had been married for five years. A widower for fifteen. It was unusual for this day and age, he knew. He'd never dated. Never even looked. His wedding ring had never left his finger in twenty years. He looked down at it now, absently twisting it around his finger. Linda had picked it out by herself and surprised him. They had been very happy together.

John was a normal, healthy man. He was terribly lonely at times. He might have been tempted to see other women if only . . . He looked up again, pretending to pay attention. If only what? he asked himself.

He didn't have any answers. Only questions. He was amazed at how fresh everything seemed. He looked towards the back of the room, where Fred was taking notes. How could that raw-boned boy, half his age, dig up all these emotions, all these memories?

Again he didn't have any answers. A very practical man, John had never been much on psychology. Still, all the issues he thought he'd resolved, all the pain he'd thought he'd worked through at Linda's death, had bobbed up from some dark, hidden place in his heart.

He suddenly realized that what he was feeling was betrayal, an overwhelming sense of betrayal. How ridiculous, he scolded himself. As if poor Linda had any choice. No, something deeper within him spoke, not Linda. You feel that God has betrayed you.

Mortified, John felt tears behind his eyes. He blinked rapidly. He hadn't cried in nearly thirty years; he couldn't possibly start now, not here! The ringing bell saved him. He dismissed the class in his usual brisk manner, only this time he rose and walked towards the window, willing his eyes to remain dry.

For a few moments Fred and John were the only ones in the room. Fred stared at the teacher in puzzlement. Since Fred had begun his education courses he'd heard the name of Mr. John Allan mentioned as the epitome of teaching. Everyone aspired to his level of calm professionalism. When Fred had first learned he was to be assigned to Mr. Allan himself, he'd been overwhelmed at what he considered to be another great blessing from God.

He had begun to wonder. Perhaps he had been placed

with Mr. Allan, not because of what Mr. Allan was, but because of what he needed. As the older man tried to surreptitiously fold and replace his handkerchief in his pocket, Fred suddenly knew he was there to teach Mr. Allan. To teach him about God.

As John turned back and faced his student teacher, he gave him a rather cold, piercing stare. Fred swallowed; this wasn't going to be easy.

"Yes, Fred? Can I help you with something?" he asked in carefully modulated tones.

Fred was prevented from answering by the arrival of several students. It was time for the last class to start. Both men gave a little sigh of relief, but for vastly different reasons.

John nodded and walked out the door.

Once the class was settled and Fred took attendance, he noticed that David Martin was absent. While he was more than a little glad that he wouldn't have to deal with the boy that day, he was puzzled. Hadn't he seen David in the cafeteria at noon?

He made a mental note to mention it to Mr. Allan, then called for the first book report. A girl named Bianca McClung raised her hand and walked to the front of the room.

Bianca was a beautiful cinnamon-skinned girl with a rather dramatic flair. She was a member of the drama team and had a tendency to overact even when she wasn't on the stage. The students called her a "Ms. Grayson wannabe." Unfortunately, she had a slight speech defect that came out whenever she was nervous. She would make a sort of "tsk" noise after every few words. But she had forced herself to overcome it with nearly complete success.

She now stood in front of the class a picture of confidence. Her note cards were resting in one hand while she gestured somewhat vigorously with the other. Her voice was clear and steady . . . then the door slammed.

Startled, the class turned as one to see David Martin stalk into the room. He rudely walked in front of Bianca then went to his seat. He threw his gym bag down beside his desk and sat down with such force that the metal feet of his desk dug grooves into the wooden floor, making a loud, screeching noise.

Badly rattled, Bianca tried to continue her book report before Fred could say anything to David. Fred closed his mouth, unsure of what to do.

"Uh . . . *Pride and Prejudice* is a . . . tsk . . . very good book." Bianca faltered, trying to go on. "The main character is . . . tsk . . . Elisabeth Bennet."

"Tsk, tsk, tsk," a voice said softly from the back of the room. Nobody laughed as Bianca turned a deep crimson red. Angry, Fred tried to identify her heckler.

"Uh . . . Elisabeth is . . . tsk . . . one of several . . . tsk . . . daughters . . ."

"Tsk, tsk, tsk," the voice came again, causing a tear to slide down Bianca's mortified face.

Fred knew that voice. Full of righteous indignation he stood up at his desk. "Bianca, please be seated," he said in a low voice. Then looking directly at David Martin, he continued. "Never, never have I seen such rude behavior from a person your age. This is inexcusable. The points . . ." Fred stopped as he noticed David's face was unaccountably lumpy.

"On top of everything else, are you eating in my class?" Fred demanded loudly, his anger overcoming his usual nervousness. David swallowed.

Fred marched back to David's desk, where he saw a very large hoagie perched behind the boy's literature book. Furious, Fred picked up the hoagie and slam-dunked it into a nearby trash can.

"Hey! That was my lunch!" David protested.

"No, that was the last straw," Fred returned. "Come with me. We're going to the office." Fred spoke with such authority that David was out of his seat and following the student teacher to the door before he knew what he was doing.

As they reached the door, Fred turned and pointed a bony finger at the class. "And no one is even so much as to think of leaving their seats, is that clear?"

Thirty heads nodded in unison.

As Fred left the room with his charge, the class was deadly silent for a few heartbeats, then they broke into spontaneous applause.

12

Every school seems to have one sport that unifies it. With Glendale High it was basketball. Even nonatheletes would go to the games to cheer on the school. The Friday of Glendale's game against Central was no exception. Students who didn't know a center from a cheerleader were wearing the school colors, eagerly looking forward to that night's game.

Only the staff and faculty were in a somber mood. They knew that no matter who won the game that night, they could still be on the picket line Monday morning.

A pep rally had been scheduled for that afternoon. That, coupled with the night's basketball game, was enough to keep the students from doing any real learning in the morning classes. John didn't mind, though. He had let Fred take the last class to the pep rally while he stayed behind and cleaned out his desk. If the strike was called tonight, he wouldn't be able to get back in on Monday.

He certainly didn't feel like doing any cheering today. In all his years of teaching, he'd never been involved in a strike. It seemed like such an ugly thing to him. He still couldn't resolve his feelings on the issues. He agreed with Loring and he agreed with Steve. Yet John knew no matter how much he had agreed with Steve he would never cross a picket line. Was that a matter of principles or a lack of courage? John shook his head; he wished he knew.

John just sat at his desk thinking. I had everything figured out. Everything laid out in a neat little pattern. My life wasn't great, but there was a lot of good in it. Now everything is all turned around. My job is uncertain, my friendship with Steve is a mess . . . then all these memories.

John sighed and shook his head again. He looked around at the room. He wondered when the janitor had last visited. It had probably been a while.

These four battered walls are my life, he thought. Maybe my life needs a little shaking up. When did my existence become this narrow? he asked himself, even though he knew the answer.

He saw an empty cardboard box on the table in the back. He rose to clean out his desk. As he approached the table, he saw some paper wedged between the back table leg and the bookcase. Curious, he bent over and picked it up.

It was a couple of pages from the Bible. It must have come from Fred's Bible the day he had dropped it on the floor. John began to straighten them out when he saw that one part of a verse on the top page had been highlighted in yellow.

"For the LORD shall be thine everlasting light, and the days of thy mourning shall be ended."

John stared at the verse, rereading it several times.

" . . . and the days of thy mourning shall be ended," he muttered to himself.

If only he could believe that. To have all the sorrow, all the mourning come to an end. But first he would have to understand why. Why Linda had died along with his child.

"Why?" he asked aloud to the four walls. They didn't answer.

He then glanced at the other page. There too was a verse highlighted in yellow.

"At the voice of thy cry; when he shall hear it, he will answer thee."

John felt a strange chill go down the back of his neck. This verse was too fitting. He carefully laid the two sheets in the bottom of the box and returned to his work at the desk.

Later that evening, John returned to the school gym to watch the game. The old gymnasium was wrapped in yards of colorful crepe paper and posters. The posters were all proclaiming a sure victory over Central High.

He had hardly made it through the gym's double doors before he was claimed by Renee Grayson.

"John! Goodness, look at you!" she exclaimed as she grasped his arm in her viselike grip. John was looking very nice that night. He wore a new beige and black cardigan over his white turtleneck shirt, along with a new pair of beige corduroys.

Renee was wearing a black leather pants suit that defied description. The red lace and satin camisole she wore under the leather jacket was hardly appropriate for a teacher. But then, John mused, most of what Renee wears is hardly appropriate for a teacher. She was tottering on red stiletto-heeled shoes as she led John to the bleachers.

"You simply must sit with me!" She tried to sound playful, but her voice was laced with desperation.

"Sure," was all John said, resigned to his fate. John took his seat beside Renee, then looked around. He saw that Audrea Givens was sitting a few seats away with some of her girlfriends. She smiled and waved as he caught her eye.

"So, Audrea, where's your partner in crime?"

Audrea smiled even brighter and pointed to the gym floor. There was Clark Nelson, suited up and practicing

101

with the rest of the team. The two long braids he wore on his head had been dyed the school colors, but other than that he looked pretty normal, for Clark.

John brightened, feeling better than he had for days. He was glad Clark had gone out for the team. Sports were good for boys like Clark; it kept them busy and hopefully, out of trouble. Despite his calm friendliness, there was a vague melancholy that had followed Clark for years. At different times, John had suspected him of possible drug use. But he'd never been certain. John was glad Steve had given this odd boy a chance to prove himself.

The school band began playing a rather off-key rendition of the "Star Spangled Banner." John smiled as he and everyone else rose to their feet.

John was still smiling as the crowd sat down again and the teams moved into position on the court. He noted with delighted surprise Clark Nelson was walking to the center circle. So Steve had made him starting center after all.

John looked across the crowded gym to where Steve was standing at the foul line. Steve caught his eye and gave him a thumbs-up gesture, causing John's smile to broaden.

The starting whistle brought everyone's attention back to center court. With a mighty leap, Clark whacked the airborne ball towards a teammate, who neatly retrieved it and hurried down the court to make a basket. A boy from Central then scooped the ball up and pounded down the other way with it. From that point on, the intensity never let up. Central would score a basket, only to have the ball whisked away to Glendale's backboard. The fans hardly sat down in the first two quarters.

Clark played very well, as did the rest of his teammates. But with his wacky hair and quirky little half smile he was the star of the game. John noticed towards the end of the second quarter, though, that he was slowing down quite a bit. John called over to Audrea.

"Clark seems tired. I guess he's not used to playing full out yet."

"I guess, but I thought he ran a couple of miles every day."

There was almost a sigh of relief from the crowd when the half-time buzzer sounded.

"Whew, I feel like I've played the game myself," John commented. "I need to get something to drink."

"Oh, John that's a lovely idea. I'll come with you." Renee was immediately on her feet.

Renee had quite a time navigating the bleachers in her high heels. She made such a show of hanging onto John that he felt himself growing red. Once they gained the floor, she still clung to him, causing no end of amusement to any students who walked by.

As they approached the concession stand, John noted a small cluster of teachers listening to a transistor radio. After John bought the soft drinks he walked over. Renee, of course, was right beside him.

"Levy results?" he asked Sarah Dunlap, who was holding the radio. She nodded grimly, one ear cocked towards the radio. Her eyes grew wide for a moment, then she shut the radio off.

"That's it," she said with finality.

"The levy didn't pass?" he asked, already knowing the answer.

Sarah only nodded.

Renee was unusually quiet as they returned to the bleachers. Not too surprisingly, with her mind occupied, she now climbed the bleachers with the agility of a mountain goat.

The game resumed at that point, but the teachers had lost all interest in it. The third quarter went by in a blur, with the teams still vying for two-point leads.

John's interest returned to the game during the fourth quarter, when Clark was placed back into the starting line-up. Obviously tired, he'd been benched during the third quarter. His absence had been keenly felt by the team.

Now with the boy's return, there seemed to be a very real chance of Glendale finally beating Central. John's eyes strayed to the sideline where Steve was nervously pacing. He wondered if Steve knew about the levy yet.

As the game progressed into the fourth quarter, the more observant in the bleachers began to sense there was something wrong with Clark.

"How could he pass off the ball like that?" John wondered aloud, after one bungled play. "There wasn't anyone near him."

John watched closely, a look of great concern on his face. He stared intently as the boy went by the stands, shuffling more than running. His eyes seemed very shiny and unfocused. John shot a look over at Audrea Givens, who was sitting white-faced with her hands to her mouth. That was all he needed.

John began to scramble down the crowded bleachers, hoping somehow to get word to Steve without causing a major scene. He had to take Clark out of the game.

Just as John reached the gym floor, a loud cry went up from the stands and John heard a sickening smack of bodies hitting the wooden floor. He pushed aside the people in front of him and saw Clark lying at the bottom of a tangle heap of players. Tears were streaming from the teenager's eyes as he clutched his arm. It was broken.

13

John watched sadly as the ambulance pulled out of the parking lot. Audrea and one of Clark's teammates, Joey Dixon, were in the back of the ambulance with Clark. John would follow later in his car, after he had hopefully contacted Clark's parents.

He walked slowly back to the building and to the school's office, the loud sound of cheering reaching his ears. The game was continuing without Clark. He had fallen and would probably face no end of trouble at the hospital, but the game was still going on. What a wonderful metaphor for life, John thought bitterly, as his footsteps echoed down the empty hallway.

It was dreadful to think of Clark huddled on the gym floor, his arm bent in a gruesome position underneath him. John knew it was a sight he would always remember.

He sighed deeply, thinking of the boy. John had always suspected Clark of drug use; he suspected it of several of his students. In Clark's case he had hoped that he might be able to steer the boy to writing or sports—anything that might guide him away from that deadly trap.

Was hoping for the best all he could do for his students? Should he have called Clark's parents over the

105

nebulous concerns he'd had? But students seldom if ever came to class totally stoned. They were a little too happy or a little too quiet. If one looked close enough their eyes might seem especially shiny. Maybe. It was all quite intangible, very hard to pin down. In the large classes he taught, how could he notice someone being too quiet? Plus, John had known several teachers to bring a host of troubles upon themselves for accusing a student of drug use. Some parents were more concerned with their family's reputation than the child's actual welfare.

John shook his head as he rounded a corner. No, he wasn't going to excuse himself. He should have been more aware; he should have known what was going on and acted accordingly. As he approached the office, John was haunted by the fact that a few years ago, he would have. When did I become blind? he asked himself.

The office seemed dark and forbidding as he searched for the light switch. It took him some time to find just one switch for a small, distant light fixture. Then he realized he had no idea what Clark's phone number was.

He looked in vain for a Rolodex or a student phone directory. Glancing at the formidable computers perched on each secretary's desk, he wished he knew more about these latest models. He had an old Apple computer at home, but it was a dinosaur compared to the gleaming new models before him. If he just knew how to turn one on he could probably call up Clark's blood type, let alone his phone number. As it was he could only stare helplessly at the dizzying array of each keyboard.

With relief, John heard the click of high heels coming down the hallway. As Renee appeared in the doorway, he could actually say he was glad to see her. He knew her to be quite adept at computers.

"Renee! Perfect timing," he greeted her warmly. "I need to call Clark's parents. I never thought to ask Audrea for the number. I don't remember his father's name, so I can't even use a phone book." He motioned to the computers. "Could you get his number from one of these?"

Renee simply beamed at his unusually enthusiastic welcome. "Well, there probably isn't any safeguard on just the student phone numbers," she said, sitting down to the nearest computer. "They usually put passwords on the more confidential records." In a matter of moments she had the computer on and was going through its menu.

In the half light of the office, the computer screen lit Renee's face in a very flattering way. Her harsh makeup job was greatly softened in the flickering light of the monitor. John watched her as she worked. He noted for the first time how large and clear her eyes were. There was something about the clean lines of her face and throat that suddenly seemed quite appealing to him.

Renee was very aware that John was looking at her. She tilted her chin up a little, then turned to him slowly.

"I have it."

"What? Oh, yes, the phone number. Great!" John stammered, embarrassed that Renee might have read his thoughts.

Renee looked at him a moment, making sure her face was still well lit by the screen. She pursed her lips in a cute little gesture and reached for his hand. "John, I know how difficult this is going to be. Would you like me to call his family?"

"Well . . ." John hesitated, torn between relief and guilt.

"I have Clark in one of my classes, too," she reminded him. "Besides, I think this is going to require a woman's touch." She gave his hand a gentle squeeze.

John's breath caught in a way he couldn't understand. After all, this was Renee! Renee Grayson, the woman he spent the better part of his working day avoiding. He nodded, letting out his breath slowly. But she was a woman and an attractive one at that.

Her eyes never left his as she picked up the phone receiver and dialed. Her voice was very calm and soothing as she spoke to the boy's mother. She tactfully made no mention of the suspicions surrounding Clark's fall. John was glad about that. The Nelsons didn't need to be told everything at one blow. Besides, there was always the off chance that Clark had just been tired and clumsy. A fat chance, John thought sadly.

"They're on their way to the hospital," Renee said returning the receiver to its cradle.

A motion in the doorway caused them both to turn. Steve Brooks stood there, his face somber and forbidding in the half light.

"You called his parents, then?" he asked coldly.

"Yes, I did," Renee returned with no greater degree of warmth.

Steve looked oddly at John then shrugged his shoulders. He turned back to the hallway without a word.

John looked with dismay at Renee, then followed Steve out to the hallway. "Steve, wait!" he called to his friend, who was already halfway down the hall.

Steve stopped and turned around very slowly. The red exit sign over a doorway cast the only light in the hall. Steve's disgruntled face didn't look any friendlier in the reddish glow.

John walked up to his friend. He wished he could close the emotional distance between them as easily.

"We lost." The words came out like two bullets and echoed down the dark hallway. "I played that freak kid of yours and we lost. We lost."

"Clark broke his arm!"

Steve didn't respond to that. He looked at John for a moment, then studied the floor. "Of all the dumb games I've ever coached I wanted this one the most. You knew that," he said in a low voice. "First you get my star player suspended, then you con me into playing some freak who

108

can't stay off the drugs for one lousy game. I knew better than to use that kid!"

John could only stare at the unfairness coming from this man. He pulled at one of the leather buttons on his cardigan, too hurt to speak.

Steve continued to address the floor. "Wake up, John. You're not the only one with problems."

Steve turned and walked out the exit, leaving John alone in the darkened hallway. Hurt beyond words, John could only stare at the door. Feeling something in his hand, he looked down to see he had torn the button right off his sweater.

With great calculation, Renee watched him from the office doorway. Her first instinct was to begin a running tirade on Steve Brooks, to commiserate with John by running Steve down. But something stopped her. Whatever Renee was, she wasn't stupid.

She had always seen John as a strong, self-reliant man, impervious to whatever charms she might possess. But as he stood there in the hallway looking at his torn sweater like a forlorn little boy, she realized how vulnerable he was. She would never get such a chance again. If she just played things right.

"He's really hurting, you know."

"What?" John looked up, confusion etched in his face.

"Oh, I'm sorry, John. I couldn't help but overhear," she said in a small contrite voice.

He made a dismissive gesture with his hand.

"That's all right. But what do you mean he's hurting?"

"Why John, you don't think he really meant those terrible things he said to you?"

"Well . . ."

"No, John. Right now, I can't imagine a better friend than Steve Brooks. Can't you see what he's doing? How he's trying to spare you?"

"Spare me?"

She moved closer to him, her eyes full of compassion and concern. She folded her arms across her chest, making sure the red light of the exit sign brought out the highlights of her satin shirt.

"John, everyone knows Steve will cross the picket lines. It's going to cause him a world of hard feelings. Knowing what a good friend you are, you might feel that you should join him out of loyalty. He wants to spare you all the grief that would cause."

He looked at her uncertainly. "Do you really think so?"

She smiled and nodded her head. "Of course," she said gently. "That's the kind of person Steve is. He's more concerned about your position and your future here at the school than he is his own." She paused, willing some moisture into her eyes. "He'll even sacrifice your friendship to safeguard your best interests." She allowed a lone tear to slip down her cheek. "I think it's just . . . the most beautiful thing I've ever seen," she whispered.

John nodded, greatly encouraged by her words. "Maybe I should call him, then? Tonight, after he gets home?"

"No . . . I wouldn't. He's going to keep pretending he's mad at you until this strike is over. You might as well go along with it." She looked intently into his eyes. "It'll be better for him, really; he won't have to be feeling guilty about dragging you down too."

"Yes, I can see that," John admitted reluctantly. Could life possibly get anymore complicated? he asked himself. He looked gratefully at Renee. "I'm glad you were here. I don't think I would have understood what Steve was trying to do."

She made a slight shrugging motion. "Woman's intuition."

He looked at her for a long moment. She seemed so different this evening, warmer, softer. Was she different? Or was he? It was totally insane for him to be thinking this way. There was too much going on in his life right now and it was clouding his judgment.

The only thing he knew for certain was how terribly alone he felt. Unbidden and unwanted, came the thought that Renee had a very different outlook on life than he did. He wouldn't have to be alone tonight.

He took a deep breath. "I'd better go. I need to get to the hospital. I didn't mean to take so long here."

"Of course."

"Thanks, Renee, thanks for everything."

She smiled warmly, watching him walk to the door. Just as his hand was on the bar, she called out. "Oh, John!"

"Yes?" He turned back a little too quickly. It spoke volumes to Renee.

"I was thinking, you have been here a while. Audrea and Joey may have already gotten a ride home. Why don't I call the hospital? There's no sense in your making the trip for nothing."

John looked out the safety glass window of the metal door for a moment, then back at Renee. She looked so inviting in the light's soft glow. A part of him knew what she was doing. A part of him didn't care.

"All right," he said slowly.

He watched her return to the office, a sense of longing welling up within him. He leaned his warm cheek against the cool metal of the door. He knew he shouldn't be lingering here; the temptation was too great.

John had never seriously dated any woman but his late wife. A moral man, he had always treated her like a lady. Out of devotion and respect he had saved the greatest depths of his love until they were married.

John was still a moral man, but tonight he felt out of kilter. Who was to say what was right or wrong? There were no absolutes anymore. Why, just last month his students had had to go to a safe sex seminar. They hadn't

111

been taught about whether it was right, only if it was safe. If this was the approach society was taking with teenagers, why should an adult be concerned? Why should he try to stand against the tide?

Fifteen years was a long, long time for a normal man to be alone. Yet in a strange way, John knew what he wanted now was more emotional than physical. There was a great gaping void that he had just lately become aware of. He ached deep inside.

As Renee walked back into the hallway he knew that he could stop the ache at least temporarily.

"It's a good thing I called. Clark's dad took Audrea and Joey home. Clark's mom is still with him in the emergency room. I got the impression they didn't want anyone else around. She seemed rather embarrassed."

"Really? I hope that doesn't mean he was on drugs, then."

Renee made a show of great concern as she shook her head.

"That poor family. That poor misguided boy. If he has taken something, I don't know how he can keep it from the doctor. Would the doctor call the police?"

"I don't know." John shook his head, depressed. "I don't know what the policy is."

"Don't forget John, that boy thinks a lot of you. No matter what happens in the days ahead, I think you could help turn him around."

John sighed and shook his head. Renee moved closer and placed both her hands on his shoulders.

"Now listen, John," she spoke softly, her head tilted down. "It was just awful what happened tonight. What happened with Clark, what happened with Steve, then to top it all off the levy fails. It's terrible, I know."

Something far in the back of his mind told John he ought to step back, keep Renee at a distance. He ignored it as she continued.

"This may be just what Clark needs to get back on track. Such a . . . public stumble may wake his parents up and get him the help he needs. Then with the strike? Well, you know it can't go on forever. And once it's over, Steve will be right back to normal."

He drank her soothing words in gratefully. They may have been the weakest platitudes, but it was so nice having someone trying to cheer him up again.

She looked up and met his gaze. "But no matter what John, I'd like for you to think of me as a . . . friend."

He was tired, he was hurting. He'd been on an emotional roller coaster for weeks now and wanted it to stop. She was very close, she was very willing. He drew her forward and kissed her.

14

Early Saturday morning John awoke with a start. Teddy had shoved his cold wet nose into his ear. John sat straight up, his heart pounding. Disoriented, he looked down to the floor where the dog was calmly watching him.

"You know I hate that," he said sternly.

Teddy merely wagged his tail.

"All right, I'm coming." John sighed. He rose from his bed and put on a robe, then padded to the front door in his bare feet. Teddy, following right behind, took the opportunity to nuzzle his bare ankles.

"Would you quit that?" John demanded as he held the door open. Teddy paused and stretched luxuriously, making an elaborate show of ignoring John and the open door. Then finally, with the greatest unconcern, he trotted out.

John stepped out on the porch to retrieve the morning paper. The single word STRIKE made up the newspaper's front-page headline. John stood in the doorway reading the article while he waited for Teddy.

The article was quite in-depth. It covered all the facts leading up to the strike and how long it was speculated to last. John let out a heavy sigh as he read it. There were issues involved that wouldn't be solved overnight.

Teddy was quite unconcerned. After cruising through the dew-soaked grass with his low-slung body, he returned to the porch. He thought drying his cold, wet fur on John's bare legs to be an especially good idea.

"Hey! Hey, you stop that!"

Teddy rolled onto his back, sticking his paws into the air, a picture of abject contrition.

"Don't give me that. You knew exactly what you were doing." John looked down at him with irritation. "Dog food, hmm? Do you want me to start giving you dog food?"

Teddy merely thumped his bushy tail, unimpressed by the threat. He knew in a matter of minutes John would fix him the same amount of eggs and toast he'd fix for himself.

John sighed yet again and held the door back open. In a fluid movement, Teddy was on his feet and briskly walking into the house. He wore a peculiar canine smile.

John followed him into the kitchen. "You think you're so smart now, but if that strike lasts too long, we may both be eating dog food."

Teddy merely lay down on his favorite throw rug, watching John take the egg carton from the refrigerator. John's preparations were interrupted by the ringing of the phone.

John moved towards it, then stopped. It could be Loring, or someone else from the union, wanting him to walk the picket line. School would not be closed on Monday. The Board of Education had been able to round up enough substitute and retired teachers to have classes. Not to mention, poor Steve would probably be there teaching.

John listened to the ringing phone. How could he face his students with a picket sign in his hands? Especially when he didn't have the courage of conviction behind him.

As the phone continued to ring, another thought occurred to him. It could be Renee. He tugged nervously on his robe's belt. What in the world was he going to do about her? He'd been very stupid last night to kiss her. Renee was the same as she always was, brash and calculating. He was the one who'd been different—tired, lonely, and stupid with a capital "S". He knew in the cold light of morning that he definitely did not want her to be a part of his life.

Teddy looked up at him.

"It's my phone, I pay the bills," John told him defensively. "I don't have to jump and answer it every time it rings."

The phone stopped ringing and John looked at it guiltily. He shrugged and began to crack eggs into the pan. When the phone began to ring again, he was startled into dropping an egg to the floor.

"Oh, forevermore! Teddy would you get that?" John pointed to the mess on the floor before he reached for the phone.

"What is it?" John demanded with asperity as he picked up the phone.

There was a long pause on the other end, then Fred's meek voice, "Uh, hi. Mr. Allan?"

"Fred! Sorry, I don't usually answer the phone so rudely. I was in the middle of something." John turned to see Teddy sniff idly at the broken egg before he returned to his rug. He liked his eggs cooked, thank you. John sighed.

"Mr. Allan, I was going to ask you . . . uh, well . . . I was wondering if you knew how long the strike would be going on?"

"No, son, I really couldn't say."

There was another long pause before Fred spoke again. "I went to the hospital as soon as I heard about Clark's injury. I think he is going to be fine."

Clark! John cursed himself; he'd forgotten all about the boy.

"Is he home? How's his arm?"

"He broke his arm in two places, but they were clean breaks. The doctor said he should heal all right, but it will take some time."

"Fred, is he home?"

"No, he won't be going home for a while. The emergency room nurse was going to give him something for his pain, but Audrea spoke up. She told her she was afraid Clark already had some drugs in his system."

"Did he?"

"Yes, he was definitely on something, but he wouldn't talk. The doctor told Clark's parents he'd keep the law out of it, if they'd agree to admit Clark to a special unit at the hospital."

"Oh, no."

"I think it's a good thing, Mr. Allan. Clark and his family need to wake up. His parents were pretty ugly to the hospital staff and Audrea."

"Audrea? Why would they be mad at her?"

"They were angry that she would even suggest Clark could be on drugs. Then they did a complete flip-flop and accused her of getting Clark on drugs in the first place."

"How awful! I should have been there."

"I had a long talk with Audrea on the phone. She was really upset, but I was finally able to show her she'd done the right thing by Clark. I think she was nearly convinced she hadn't betrayed him by the time I picked them up and took them home."

"I don't understand. I was told Clark's father had taken Audrea and Joey home."

"No, sir. The Nelsons made it very clear they didn't want any of them around. So Audrea called me and I came to the hospital."

John was silent, amazed that Renee could lie so easily.

"I'm sorry, Fred. I was coming to the hospital, but I received some wrong information. I certainly didn't mean to leave Audrea and Joey stranded."

"Don't worry about it, Mr. Allan. I think this might all be a blessing in disguise. Clark has a chance to get turned around, and Audrea even agreed to come to church Sunday."

"So, I wondered when you would start evangelizing my students. Will Sunday school keep her from eternal damnation?"

The silence on the phone made John immediately regret his sarcasm. "Fred, that was pretty uncalled for. I'm sorry, I'm sure you mean well."

"That's okay, Mr. Allan. I understand."

"Do you? I wish I did. Well, I hope you get to finish your student teaching. Fred, keep in touch."

"Mr. Allan . . ."

"Good-bye, son." John hung up before the boy could say anything more. He certainly didn't want the boy to invite him to church. He had a very strong suspicion that Fred had intended that very thing.

John felt terrible about Clark. Fred had certainly stood by him better than he had. He wondered if Clark would be allowed visitors. He'd have to call and find out.

After John had cleaned up the mess on the floor and fixed breakfast, he wondered how to spend the rest of the day. He couldn't bear to think about lesson plans. The idea of running errands didn't appeal to him either. There were too many people in his little town that he wanted to avoid just now.

Cleaning, that was the ticket. Some mindless menial labor would be just the thing. He decided his long-neglected basement deserved the most immediate attention.

John had never been a casual jean-and-t-shirt type of person. He managed to look rather presentable even when cleaning out the depths of a basement. Not that there was some horrible mess to clean up. John would never allow anything to get too disheveled. He did accumulate things, though. He could attach sentiment to the most mundane items, making it nearly impossible to throw them away.

He was now faced with boxes and boxes of memories. The upstairs of his house was rather bare, but down in the basement he kept a lifetime of flotsam and jetsam.

Armed with garbage bags and more empty boxes, he resolved to throw away some things and pack off at least a couple of boxes worth to the Goodwill Store.

"I don't need all this stuff," he addressed Teddy, who had stationed himself in the seat of an old metal lawn chair. "Isn't that seat cold?"

Teddy didn't seem to think so but watched intently for any tidbits that might come his way.

The first box that John opened contained ten years worth of grade books. He picked up one and began to rummage through it.

"Now, why would anyone keep all these grade books? Ew, there's David Martin's grades. I suppose I should keep these in case his parents try to bring a malpractice suit against me. No, I'll just have to rely on my charm, eh Ted?"

Teddy looked dubious, but John threw the grade books into a trash bag anyway. He plowed through the next two boxes with resolve, even throwing away the pair of tennis shoes he'd worn in his last high school basketball game. He held them lovingly for a moment, just out of reach of the all-consuming trash bag.

"I used to surprise them, Teddy. I didn't have the height, but I could fly. I'd have a good four feet between me and the floor. Well, all right, maybe it was more like three feet, but I was still in the air." He laughed softly to himself. "They used to call me the Flying Bookworm. I was the only player to have read the complete works of Shakespeare."

He hesitated a moment longer, then tossed them into the trash bag, saying, "Parting is such sweet sorrow."

John pressed on until late afternoon, making several determined trips to the garbage cans out back. Each trip cost him a little, but they became progressively easier. Finally, there were only five boxes unopened. They seemed to huddle forlornly against the back wall. He stared at them a long moment.

"This would be a good time to quit," he announced. Teddy opened one of his closed eyes then returned to his nap. All this rummaging and he had yet to see any sign of a snack.

John stood over the boxes, just looking. Each one had been carefully sealed, then double-wrapped in plastic. They looked as if they weren't supposed to be opened. When he had packed them fifteen years ago, he really hadn't meant to open them again.

He placed a hand on the largest box. It was nearly four feet across and very heavy. He idly traced the word "nursery" with his index finger. No, there was no need to open this one. He remembered vividly the disassembled white furniture and delicate curtains and bedding. He and his wife had spent months picking everything out. What a shame none of it had ever been used.

Preserved as carefully as museum pieces, John knew everything within would be as clean and crisp as the day he had packed it away. It suddenly seemed such a waste for it all to go unused. How many expectant couples would love to have such an ensemble?

He stood thinking and remembering for a few minutes before he came to a decision. He took a fat, black marker from his pocket and crossed the word "nursery" out. Underneath he wrote "Goodwill." He looked at his handwriting for a moment, then unaccountably a small smile stole across his face. Yes, he did have "goodwill." It was pleasant to think that some young couple could use all the nice baby furnishings within. His smile grew larger as he pictured some happy couple bringing their baby home to a well-fitted nursery. He really liked the idea that he could contribute to some unknown baby's homecoming.

He was more than a little surprised at himself. Where was the sorrow, the bitterness, that always accompanied thoughts of his lost child? It was still there, he knew. But just for today the internal clouds had parted a little. After fifteen years of hoarding a room full of baby things he decided it was time to give it away.

After wrestling the cumbersome box out the basement door and into his van, John returned to the house to wash up. A glance at his watch assured him there was plenty of time before the Goodwill Store would close.

He felt better than he had in days. It was so strange that this little act of generosity could have such an impact on him. Was it possible? Could he finally be starting to heal?

15

A small bell chimed over his head as he pushed the door open. John looked around the store curiously. The Goodwill Store was housed in an old warehouse, its walls running at irregular angles. There were large bins of used clothing with neat hand-printed signs overhead. He smiled as he saw the racks of men's suits lining one wall. They represented every style from the last fifty years.

"May I help you?"

John turned to see a small blond woman behind the counter. He smiled at her. "Nothing's changed," he said.

"Excuse me?"

He continued to smile as he walked to the counter. "When my wife and I were first married we did all our shopping here. This and the grocery store were the only places we could afford to go." He pointed to a doorway. "There used to be floor to ceiling bookcases in there. I'd fill paper bags full of secondhand books. It made Linda a little crazy."

The woman laughed, nodding her head. "My husband and I did all our shopping here, too. I guess it's only fitting I ended up working here. You'd better warn your wife, though, the books are still there."

John let the remark go, not feeling the need to relate his wife's death. It seemed to be all he was thinking about lately, and today he just wanted to be positive.

"Well, I've brought something in return for all those wonderful books. I have a huge box of baby things out in the van that I thought might do someone some good."

"Do you?" the woman positively beamed. "I know of a young couple who would love to have anything at all for their baby. Do you need help bringing it in? My son is coming by to help stock; he'll be here any minute."

Her enthusiasm warmed him, encouraging him that he had made the right decision. He smiled again. "I can manage. I'll be right back."

In a few minutes, John had wrangled the box into the store, pushing it to the left of the counter. The little woman was right beside him, eager to help as he carefully removed each item from the box. He was glad she was there; it eased everything somehow.

They removed the unassembled baby bed first. How long it had been since he'd sanded and painted it! He ran a loving hand across the whimsical decals on its side. Linda had put them there.

The woman's bright green eyes twinkled with curiosity as she looked up at John. He seemed too old to have babies of his own, but a little too young for grandchildren. There was a story here, she just knew it.

"You know," he began softly. "I'd forgotten, but we bought this bed here. It was the ugliest thing, all brown and dented."

She shook her head in wonder as she looked at the beautiful white paint and delicate gold trim.

John began pulling packages wrapped in plastic out of the box, while the woman carefully unwrapped each item and placed them on the counter.

"Goodness, but this is wonderful. Look at all these nice things. It certainly looks like they've been carefully preserved. This is like Christmas . . ." she gushed, then stopped with a blush. "Oh, you must think I'm silly going on like this."

He thought she was adorable but he didn't say so. She was built on a very small scale, about his age. Her green eyes tilted up slightly, giving her a pixie look when she laughed, which was something she did often.

She had a wealth of blond hair that she wore pulled up and back in a very attractive fashion. She raised a delicate hand to it now as he continued to gaze at her silently.

"This couple . . . they're very young," she faltered, suddenly shy.

"I'm glad," John assured her, then after a moment he was struck by how absurd that sounded. "I mean, I'm glad all this will be put to good use." He was starting to feel a little shy himself.

"They've made some mistakes, but they're trying to do the right thing now. I've been looking for a way to encourage them. This will be just the thing." She blushed again in a very appealing way. "I'm sorry, this must be boring you."

"No, not at all. This is just what I wanted, to help some young couple out." He bent towards the box again. "There that's . . . no, I missed something." He reached down to pick up a tiny bundle. Curious, he unwrapped it, instantly regretting it.

He stared down at a tiny pair of red and black tennis shoes. How could he have forgotten? It had been the very first thing he'd bought. He could still hear Linda's delighted laughter as he had placed them in her hands.

The woman was silent as she watched his stricken face. She thought she understood now why he had all these things.

"I'm sure you'll want to keep those," she gently said after a long pause.

He nodded, blinking a few times as he carefully placed them inside his jacket.

"Well, let me write you out a receipt," she told him as she moved back behind the counter.

"A receipt?" he asked, coming out of his reverie.

She smiled up at him. "I'll give Uncle Sam his due, but not a penny more. You're donating some very nice items there. You can use this receipt as proof of a charitable donation. Every little bit helps at tax time, I know." An accountant's mind in a pixie's body, he thought to himself. "Thank you, Mrs. . . ."

"Oh, just call me Agnes."

"Agnes, then," he smiled at her warmly, taking the receipt. "Agnes is one of my favorite characters in one of my favorite books."

"*David Copperfield?*"

His eyebrows nearly crawled off his forehead, putting his eyes in a very attractive light. "Yes! I was beginning to wonder if I'd ever run into a fellow Dickens fan again."

"Oh, yes! *David Copperfield* is my favorite, with *Bleak House.*"

"*Bleak House? Bleak House?* Nobody reads that!" John blurted out, forgetting himself. "Oh! How rude of me," he added meekly.

She only laughed again, shaking her head. "I'm used to that reaction, and I no longer feel the need to defend myself. I . . ."

They both turned their heads as the bell over the door rang, and a large family came in.

"You have customers."

"Yes," she agreed, suddenly shy again.

He lingered at the counter a moment longer, for one more harmless glimpse at her green eyes.

"Well . . . Agnes, I guess I'll be going."

"Yes, thanks again."

John left the store smiling, but a wave of depression hit him as soon as he gained the sidewalk.

"She's married," he said glumly to himself.

Within the store Agnes Evans was also feeling a little depressed. He's married, she reminded herself as she waited on her customers.

John berated himself as he drove towards home. First Renee, now I'm attracted to married women. What am I doing? Becoming some womanizer? The last thought was so absurd that he had to chuckle to himself. Let's not get carried away, John, he told himself. You only kissed Renee, and finding a woman to be cute, even very cute, is not a major character flaw. Cute?

The entire evening stretched before him. He really hated the thought of going home. For years he had thought of his home as a sanctuary, a retreat, but lately it had begun to seem too empty to him.

He suddenly thought of Clark Nelson and wondered if he could have visitors. His parents might not like it, he told himself. He recalled the few occasions he had seen the Nelsons; they had struck him as pretty intimidating.

"I can be rather intimidating, too," he said aloud, resolving to at least try to see the boy. He turned a corner and began to drive towards the hospital. He wondered what he would say to Clark, "Uh, you know, you really shouldn't take drugs?" Of course, the boy knew that.

John shook his head. He couldn't understand it. Clark had everything going for him. It couldn't be peer pressure, the reason so many kids took drugs. Clark never cared what anyone thought about him. He was a pleasant young man, but he had made it clear he didn't need anyone's acceptance or approval.

Everyone liked Clark, even though he had no real friends. Clark and Audrea dated, but John knew that it was pretty one-sided. Audrea was a very affectionate and loyal girl who obviously cared deeply for Clark. John was afraid she was investing in a losing proposition. Clark was a true loner. Maybe that was why John understood him so well.

As John entered the lobby, he walked up to the large hospital directory on the wall. He found the floor for the Drug Rehabilitation Unit then took the elevator. When he gained the correct floor and left the elevator, he saw there was a large empty waiting room with a desk to one side. Everything seemed to be in shades of gray. Even the nurse seated at the station in the corner wore a slate gray sweater. It matched the gray of her hair. Truth to tell, it even matched the gray tones of her flaccid skin.

The nurse looked up from where she sat behind the desk. She didn't smile.

An imposing metal door was behind and to the right of her desk. It had a small window with wire mesh set in the door's upper half. There was an intercom set in the wall beside the door. The door gave the whole place a very prisonlike atmosphere.

Poor Clark, John thought to himself as he walked towards the desk.

"Yes?" The nurse put a world of emphasis into that one word. Boredom, disdain, and just a trace of suspicion permeated it. She'd been writing something on a chart. After she pierced John with a look of her cold gray eyes, she returned to her writing.

"One of my students is in the rehabilitation program. I was wondering if I could see him?"

"One of your students?" It sounded like an accusation. She didn't look up again but continued to write.

"That's right."

"He's not your son, or an immediate family member, but one of your students?" She conveyed a tone of profound displeasure as she continued her all-absorbing epistle.

"That's right."

She was silent for a while after that. John began to idly count the gray hairs in her bent head. He was prepared to wait out her rudeness. Absolute power corrupts absolutely, he reminded himself.

128

When she saw that he wasn't going away she sighed deeply and demanded, "Name?"

"Clark Nelson."

She looked him in the eye and stood up. She was quite a bit taller than him and much, much heavier. She looked him over with a smirk as if her greater bulk somehow made her superior. "He may not want any visitors."

John regarded her calmly. He'd come to terms with his stature years ago.

When she saw that she wasn't going to be able to stare him down, she turned with a huff to the intercom behind her. She stabbed a button with a stubby finger and barked "Visitor, nonfamily!"

A metallic sounding voice asked, "Patient?"

"Nelson!"

"Just a minute."

The nurse plopped back down into her chair and began to write again. John had apparently ceased to exist for her.

The metal door opened, revealing a large, burly orderly. He had coal black eyes that seemed intent on boring a hole through people. His white uniform seemed a little dingy, as if it had picked up the grayness of the surroundings.

He was also one of the hairiest men John had ever seen. His arms were covered with thick black fur. He sported a dense black beard that grew down his neck and reached into the man's shirt.

The orderly was of the same mind as the nurse. He looked John over suspiciously, then opened the door just wide enough for him to enter. "Room 201," the man grunted.

"Thank you." John smiled up at him, determined not to have his mood dictated by this forbidding pair.

The man followed John down the hall for a few yards then veered right to take his seat at a duty station. The ward looked just like any other hospital unit, with the glaring difference that there were bars on all the windows.

John found the room, and after rapping on the open door, he entered. The bed nearest the door was empty, with Clark seated on the bed by the window. His back was to John, and despite his height, he seemed very small and forlorn.

"Clark?" John said softly.

Clark didn't turn around but continued to stare out the barred window. "'Lo, Mr. A," he returned in a small, sad voice.

Pulling a chair up to the foot of the bed, John studied Clark's pale face for a moment. The boy's two cheerfully colored dreadlocks now only accented his pallor.

The boy wore his arm in a sling over the cut sleeve of an expensive-looking sweat suit. It occurred to John for the first time that Clark's family was wealthy. One could never tell by the way the boy dressed at school. But to get him in a rehab unit like this probably took some money and connections.

"That nurse and orderly make quite a pair out there. I think they were trying to scare me," John began.

"We call 'em King Kong and Godzilla. We're taking bets as to who would win in a showdown." A little smile lifted Clark's voice, but he still refused to look at John.

The light from the setting sun streamed through the window, casting a gloomy shadow of bars across the young man's form. John wondered what could be done to keep these hospital bars from someday becoming prison bars.

They sat for a moment in silence. Clark was in his own little world, and John had no idea how to reach him.

"Why?" Clark finally said. "That's what you want to know, isn't it? That's what you're always asking in class?" There wasn't a trace of bitterness or disrespect in his voice. He spoke in a quiet monotone as he stared steadfastly out the window. "Why would a bright boy like me, from a good home, take drugs?"

"All right, Clark. Why? You've got . . ."

"Everything going for me," the boy finished, just a hint of sarcasm creeping into his voice now. "Everything money could buy."

John was prevented from answering by a bustle out in the hallway. He looked up to see the orderly entering with a burst of color that could only be Clark's mother. A well-dressed, middle-aged woman wearing a scarlet coat and a rainbow scarf, she demanded attention. Clark however, never turned around.

The hirsute orderly had been transformed by a rather phony-looking smile. He ushered the woman in with a flourish. "There you go, Mrs. Nelson! I hope you have a nice visit with your son. He's such a pleasant young man." He made an odd little bow with his massive head before retreating to his duty station.

The woman ignored the orderly as she fastened her sights on John. She pressed her thin lips into a tight line of displeasure. She was not happy to see him. "Mr. Allan," she said formally, clipping off the syllables.

Rising from his chair, John extended his hand. He wondered what was bothering Clark's mother. "Hello, Mrs. Nelson. I just came by to see how Clark was doing."

Mrs. Nelson allowed John to shake her hand then dropped it like some dead thing. Her blue eyes were two ice chips set in a face of stone. "I wonder whether Clark should have a lot of visitors just now. He's been through a lot, you know, and I wouldn't want him tired out."

John was angled in such a position that he could see both Clark's face and Mrs. Nelson's. The boy made no response to her or her words.

"In fact, Mr. Nelson was going to come by, but he was of the same mind: Clark doesn't need too many visitors."

Some indefinable expression fleeted across Clark's face, John noted, then it was gone again.

"So he went ahead and left?" Clark asked the window.

Mrs. Nelson moved hesitantly towards Clark. She almost laid a hand on his thin shoulder, but she changed her mind and hid it in the folds of her beautiful red coat. "We've been all through this, Clark," she said firmly, back in control now. "These business trips are very important. Airlines don't reschedule flights according to our little whims."

"Of course not, Mother."

"Your father has all sorts of people depending on him." She turned to address John. "Mr. Nelson takes his duties very seriously."

"He has his priorities straight," Clark said in a quiet, singsong fashion, as if he were quoting an oft-repeated phrase.

"That's right, he's . . ." Mrs. Nelson stopped as she caught the irony in Clark's voice. She looked with profound displeasure at the boy's back, then continued to speak to John. "Clark is too young to understand all the work involved with owning a growing business. We can't get him to see that some sacrifices have to be made in order to be successful."

John saw that Clark never changed his expression, though now there were two spots of pink on his pale cheeks. Focusing on the hard-faced woman before him, John was unsure of what to say.

"In any case," she said imperiously, "If you'd like to say your goodbyes, I'll wait for you out in the hall." She turned on her fashionable leather heel and left the room.

John watched her go, then let out a long sigh.

"I think Godzilla and King Kong have met their match," Clark said softly, looking at John for the first time.

16

It was with the greatest reluctance that John followed Mrs. Nelson's trail of perfume out into the hallway. A battle-scarred veteran of years of parent-teacher conferences, he could smell a bad confrontation a mile away.

His instincts were right on target; the woman turned on him as soon as he approached.

"Mr. Allan," she began primly. "I really must question the wisdom of your coming here. I fail to see any good coming of it."

"I was concerned."

"Really?" She crossed her arms and looked at him hard. "I'm sure you can understand how embarrassing this is to our family. We really don't need a bunch of people up here satisfying their morbid curiosity."

"Morbid curiosity? Clark is one of my favorite students. I was worried about him!" John fought to keep his tone low and neutral. It was hard.

"Well then, Mr. Allan, I'm sure you're not interested in all our little family arguments. Suffice it to say, Clark seems to think he doesn't get enough attention, so he likes to pull little tricks like this once in a while to get it." She noted the look on his face. "Oh please, Mr. Allan, don't act so innocent. You'd think you were the only teacher Clark has, the way he goes on about you. I'm sure Clark has poured out all his troubles to you, told you how terribly neglected and misunderstood he is."

"Actually, he never mentions his family."

Her carefully plucked eyebrows rose high over eyes thick with mascara. She made an "Oh" with her mauve lips. She was very surprised. "That's news to me. I assumed he went running to you every time he had one of these episodes."

"Episodes?"

"Didn't you know? He's been here before." She opened her purse, looked sourly at a package of cigarettes, then shut the small bag with a snap. "Grant you, he's never made such a show of himself before. Oh no, this one will make the papers," she ended bitterly.

"I didn't know," John said miserably.

"It's a neat little bit of emotional blackmail. Everything is supposed to come to a grinding halt when Clark gets his nose out of joint. But he might as well learn now the world doesn't revolve around him. He needs to get his priorities straight."

"Are you so sure you have your priorities straight?" The words were out before he could stop them.

Mrs. Nelson drew herself up and clasped her purse tightly. She stared at him with eyes of pure poison. "You're a bachelor, aren't you?" she asked sarcastically. "Of course you know all there is to raising children?"

John considered being calm and professional. He considered letting the remark pass–for about two heartbeats. "You're a mother, aren't you?" he returned quietly. "Of course you know when your child needs you?"

Her face became an ugly mask of cold fury as she stared at him. Without another word, she turned and left him standing in the hallway.

"Happy families are all alike, unhappy families are each miserable in their own way!" John quoted aloud to himself.

Turning, he saw the orderly glaring at him from the duty station. He must have been watching the whole exchange.

"That's Tolstoy I was quoting. You should read him sometime," John told him pleasantly, before he walked out the door.

John worried about Clark all the way home. He wondered what the end of it all would be. Sighing, John wished he had had some words of encouragement for the young man, some hope to offer him. "I don't have any hope to offer myself," John said bleakly within the empty van.

"And the days of thy mourning shall be ended." The comforting words suddenly came to John, making him sit up straighter. Now whatever made me think of that? John asked himself. Oh yes, those pages of Fred's Bible. I need to get them back to him. "And the days of thy mourning shall be ended," John said the words aloud, liking the sound of them.

As John pulled the van in front of his house a thought occurred to him. He had never read the Bible, not in any form. He knew it was considered to be a great work of literature. As an English teacher I really ought to put my prejudice aside and just look at it, he told himself. It might be interesting. Besides, he told himself, I really hate one of my student teachers to be so knowledgeable about a book I haven't even read.

Opening the front door, John's attention was immediately claimed by his cheerful little dog. As always, Teddy acted like his master had been gone for days instead of hours. John allowed Teddy to properly express his great joy, then stood on the porch while the dog stretched his legs running about the yard. As he waited, John leaned against the porch balustrade and thought of more of the Bible verse.

"For . . . for what? . . . The Lord shall be . . . thine . . .

thine everlasting light, and the days of thy mourning shall be ended."

Looking up at the clear night sky, John thought of the words written so long ago. They were really lovely, as lovely as the glittering stars overhead. They also offered something he wanted, something he wanted to offer Clark. Hope.

"If only they weren't just empty words," he whispered to the night.

The sound of the ringing phone caused him to jump. Recovering himself, he called to the dog. "Come on, boy. We're being paged."

Teddy scampered onto the porch and followed him into the kitchen.

"Mr. Allan?" a voice asked uncertainly when he picked up the receiver.

"Yes, this is he."

"Well! I found you on the first try! What luck! Oh! This is Agnes, from the Goodwill Store."

John felt a rather silly smile coming across his face. She's married, he told himself sternly, trying to squelch the smile.

"Mr. Allan?" she asked uncertainly at his silence.

"Sorry, Agnes. I was just . . . woolgathering." Woolgathering, what a stupid thing to say! he berated himself.

"I'm sure you're wondering why I called. I found something among all the baby things, that I wasn't sure you wanted to donate. I mean, did your wife really want to donate her Bible?"

"What?" John demanded as he stared at the receiver in his hand.

It was Agnes's turn to be silent now, as she tried to understand John's strange tone of voice.

"Agnes, did you say her Bible?"

"Yes, it's just beautiful, with such a lovely protective

cover. I thought she might have placed it with the baby things by mistake. I thought you'd want to ask her if she wanted it back."

"I can't imagine how it got in that box," John said uncertainly.

"Well, tell her not to worry. I'll keep it safe until she can come by the store and get it."

"You don't understand, Agnes. My wife died fifteen years ago in a car crash. That Bible had been right beside her when she died. I always assumed, no, I was sure it was destroyed in the accident. I have no idea . . . I don't see how it could have been in that box."

Agnes was silent again as she digested all that he told her. She looked down at the Bible she was holding in her lap. As she traced the delicate embroidery on the cover, she wondered at the history of this particular Bible. She also wondered what further uses lay in store for it. He's not married, she couldn't help but think.

"John, I don't know what you believe," she finally said. "But I think someone has gone to a great deal of trouble to keep this Bible safe for you. I know everything has a purpose and there must be a reason why it's coming back into your life at this time."

"Well, I have to admit, if I'd seen it right after the accident I would have chucked it into the nearest trash can." He paused a moment before asking rather timidly, "I hope that doesn't shock you."

She smiled broadly at the little-boy quality in his voice. "I think God understands anger. I think He also understands honest questions. I know I had plenty when my husband died."

There was a full minute's silence on the line before John could work up the courage to ask. "Oh, when your first husband died?"

"I was speaking of my only husband; I'm a widow."

John felt his silly grin returning, and this time he

didn't try to stop it. She's not married. "I'm sorry, Agnes, I know how difficult it can be."

"Thank you."

"Agnes, maybe I can come by the shop tomorrow and pick it up?" John said hesitantly. "I think Linda would have wanted me to keep it. She was very fond of it." John found that he had to switch the hand holding the receiver. His palms had become unaccountably sweaty.

"Of course," she agreed kindly. "But the store's closed on Sundays. How about Monday?"

"Will you be there? Uh, I mean will somebody be there?"

"Sure, nine to five!"

His face was starting to ache from his ear to ear smiling.

"Good, then. That will be good. Monday. I'll see you Monday. Yes, thank you. I'll see you Monday." Aware that he was starting to babble slightly, John decided he'd better ring off. "Good night, Agnes."

"Good night, John," she responded warmly.

After placing the receiver back, John bent down and gently lifted Teddy's face to his own. "She's not married," he whispered to the dog.

Teddy seemed to understand.

17

John spent that Sunday morning as he spent all Sunday mornings. He read the paper on the front porch, while Teddy investigated every nook and cranny of the yard.

He wore a sweater that morning, noting with regret that it would soon be too cold to sit outside. In the early morning quiet he could hear the sound of distant church bells calling people to service—a lovely sound that he'd never really paid much attention to before.

Putting his paper down, he held his head up and just listened. The bells were nice and soothing. He wondered which church they came from. Linda's old church? He remembered going there with her a few times. It hadn't been nice and soothing like the churches he had known. The preacher hadn't tried to placate the people with a lofty, sonorous sermon.

He leaned back in his wicker chair, remembering. No, it definitely hadn't been nice and soothing, he chuckled. The preacher had wanted to stir things up, to make people responsible for their own actions. "You are accountable!" He could recall the man saying, or yelling rather.

He'd found it to be disturbing, but exciting too. He'd had to think at that church, not fight against sleep. Smiling, he remembered the music. That he had enjoyed immensely. There'd been a youth choir led by a teenage girl. What was her name? Jessica, that was it. She'd really done a job with that choir. They'd sounded as good as any adult choir he'd ever heard.

Linda had loved those kids in the choir. He wondered if any of them still went there. Fifteen years was such a long time. Would there be anyone there who remembered her? Who remembered how much she'd cared?

He found himself suddenly curiously nostalgic. What would it be like to go to one service? I could sit in the back by the door. I could leave anytime I wanted to. Nobody would know who I was.

He shrugged and dismissed the errant thought. Sure, right, he told himself as he continued to read his paper. He read a few more articles in a desultory fashion, but his mind wasn't really on what he was reading.

Sitting forward, he fingered the paper in his lap. If I sat all the way in the back, right by the door, I could just listen to the choir. It'd be a little rude but I could even leave before the sermon started.

He smiled at the thought and began to look through the sports section. The Glendale game was there with only the slightest mention of Clark. The paper treated his fall as an unfortunate accident, that was all. Good, the boy had enough problems.

John looked down to the slacks he was wearing. Never a slouch in his dress, what he had on was very presentable. You know, I could throw on a tie, change this sweater for a jacket, he mused, looking at his watch. This is crazy, he told himself. But if I sat in the very back . . .

His reverie was interrupted by the slamming of a car door. He looked up to see Renee waving at him from the gate. She was trying to open the gate, but Teddy in his excitement kept jumping up and pushing it closed.

"Smart dog," he murmured to himself. He returned Renee's wave and left the porch.

"John! What an adorable dog! He's such a cutie!" Renee beamed at him as she tried to open the gate.

"Hi, Renee, here I'll get him. Back Teddy, get back, boy." John pulled Teddy back long enough for Renee to get into the yard, but as he bent to relatch the gate, Teddy wriggled free and jumped up on Renee. Renee squealed as the dog's claws left several jagged runs in her yellow jersey dress.

"You miserable . . . I mean, mischievous little dog," she muttered, trying hard to control her temper.

John swept Teddy into his arms, while he stared in dismay at Renee's ruined dress.

"I'm so sorry! He's never done anything like that before," he told her while Teddy gleefully licked his face. Teddy didn't seem in the least sorry.

"Here, come on in, Renee, I'll put the dog up." John had meant come on into the yard, thinking they could sit on the porch, but he found Renee was right behind him, following him into the house while he struggled with the dog.

Fearing she might follow him even to the bedroom, John nodded towards the living room. "Have a seat on the couch while I lock this fellow up."

Teddy gave John's face another lick before he set him down. "We will talk later, young man," John told him sternly.

Teddy only grinned and thumped his tail.

John returned to the living room to find Renee perched rather dramatically on the arm of the couch. She had recovered her aplomb despite the runs in her dress and, John now saw, a few in her hose.

"Again, I'm so sorry." John spread out his hands, making sure to take a seat on the far side of the small room. "Let me at least replace the cost of the dress."

"What, this old thing?" Renee made a dismissing gesture across the dress she had just bought yesterday, bought especially to impress him. "Don't think twice about it. I'm glad your cute little dog . . . likes me," she finished lamely.

"I insist; I'll make it up to you." John looked speculatively at the dress, figuring it would cost at least half a paycheck.

She misinterpreted his gaze completely. Running a hand through her hair, she smiled at him coyly. "Well, I'm glad to see that you like it," she murmured.

"Oh!" His gaze switched quickly to her face and locked there. "Yes," he said blushing, "It's really very nice. Very pretty."

She leaned back and gave John a side long look. "John, you don't need to be embarrassed with me. Not after the other night. I was hoping you'd find the dress . . . and me, to be attractive."

"Right, of course, well . . . so Renee, have you heard anything about the strike?"

She dropped the femme fatale role and sat straight up. She was suddenly all business. "Yes, I talked to Calvin Loring last night. He wants all of us teachers to meet in front of the school at 7:30 in the morning. Word is, the district is going to try and bus in some substitute teachers from out of the county. We need to be there as a show of strength."

"A show of strength?"

"That's right. We're to form a picket line straight across the entrance of the school."

"Can we stop people from entering?"

"No, not legally. But we don't have to make it easy for the scabs."

"Goodness, that's such an ugly word."

Renee shrugged unconcernedly. "You're too kind-hearted, John. They're undermining everything we're trying to do. Then if we do win any concessions, they'll share in the victory the same as the teachers who went out on strike."

"That's true, I know, but what if they don't really believe we should have a strike at all? What if it's a matter of principles?"

"Principles," she snorted. "I don't think so. Let's say a matter of making as much money as possible. Not to mention brownie points with the board."

"What about the students? Will they be going to school only to see their teachers shouting and waving signs about?"

"Oh, John, they understand what we're doing this for. The students will benefit as much as any of us."

He frowned, thinking that over. There was a lot of truth in what she was saying. Still, why did it just feel so wrong?

"Such a long face!" she cooed, "I didn't come here to make you unhappy." She smiled sassily at him, back in her enchantress mode. "I thought we could talk about the other night."

John felt completely out of his element. He'd known he was going to have to talk to Renee, but he'd thought he'd be better prepared for it.

"Yes . . . about the other night," he began uncertainly.

Renee got up from the couch and walked over to him. She planted a kiss right on top of his head, before she sat down on the chair's arm, apparently a favorite spot for her.

"There, that's a little payback for the best kiss I ever had."

John blushed to the few roots of his hair, while Renee oblivious to his true emotions, leaned back and draped an arm across his shoulder.

"Renee . . . there's been a lot going on in my life lately. A lot!"

"I know, dear," she murmured.

"I'm not sure you do. I can't really explain it all. This business with the strike, then Clark. Not to mention everything that's been happening with my student teacher. In fact, I can't really discuss it because I still haven't sorted all of that out."

"I'm sure it's been just terrible," she agreed as she ran a finger over the back of his ear.

"Yes, well . . . what I'm trying to say is that the other night was especially confusing. I don't think . . . in fact, I know it was wrong to kiss you like I did. To kiss you at all."

Renee saw where this was going and she didn't like it one bit. "Wrong?" she asked in a small voice.

"You're a fine person, Renee; you were being very kind to me. The way I reacted was more physical than emotional. I'm sorry. I didn't mean to take advantage of your friendship."

Laughing softly, Renee tilted John's head towards her. She was on firmer ground now. "You're too sweet. It was just a kiss. How is that taking advantage of me?"

John looked at her sadly, thinking that she could never really understand him. "Because Renee, I didn't mean it. I was lonely, tired, depressed . . . but whatever I felt, it wasn't the right emotion to build anything with." He continued in a softer tone. "I didn't have the right to kiss you because I don't feel anything for you. Not in the way you want me to."

In a single smooth movement Renee removed her arm from his shoulder and stood to her feet. "Not in the way I want you to?" she asked archly.

"Well, I know you've been attracted to me. I think you might have hoped I'd feel the same," he said kindly.

She assumed a slight, condescending smirk as she looked down at him. She placed her hands on her hips for a moment, then began to closely study the fingernails of her right hand. "Oh, John, you're being a bit presumptu-

144

ous aren't you?" She spoke in carefully casual tones. "I don't want you to feel anything."

"Honestly, someone shows you a little sympathy, a little pity really, and you jump to all sorts of conclusions." She smoothed her skirt down in a few quick, nervous gestures before she looked at him. "You don't for one minute think that kiss meant anything to me, do you?"

"Well . . ."

"As the kids say, 'Get a life, John,'" she said with growing irritation. "I was going to try and stop you, only I felt so bad for you. I figured I was the first woman you'd kissed in years. Believe me, I had no idea it was going to go to your head like this."

John had always thought Renee could get really ugly once she got started. He looked at her calmly, no longer feeling sorry for her.

"I think that might be a good place to stop," he said, rising to his feet.

"Do you?" her voice was taking on a shrill tone. "Well, let me tell you, John Allan, if you weren't so busy mooning over ghosts you might know what to do with a real woman when you had one!"

A number of retorts came to him, but he bit them off and simply stared at her. She tilted her head up in a defensive gesture and walked out the front door, and yes, she did slam it shut.

"Well, that could have gone better," John told himself.

He sat down again drained. Putting his face in his hands he realized that he had been told off by three different people in as many days. "I'm really not a popular fellow," he told the floor. "This definitely isn't my week."

Sighing he went to the bedroom and let Teddy out. "I suppose I should be mad at you."

Teddy didn't seem to think so. Instead he looked longingly at the front door.

"Our theatrical friend has exited stage right," he told

the dog. "But you can go out while I rustle us up some lunch."

After letting Teddy out, John returned to the kitchen, wondering if anything else could possibly go wrong. A strike, Steve mad, Clark in the hospital, Renee mad . . . well, that last was almost inevitable, he reasoned. At least Renee knew once and for all how he felt.

His natural good humor tried to reassert itself as he got ready for lunch. He probably should have applauded when she left. There was quite a bit of acting in that dramatic scene.

Resolving the situation with Renee also cleared the way for other possibilities. John smiled as he set a pitcher of tea on the table. Agnes. Did I just meet her yesterday? What a funny little name. "But a rose is a rose by any other name," he told the silverware as he removed it from the drawer.

It would be nice to see her tomorrow. Could I ask her to dinner? Would that be too soon? he wondered. Maybe lunch, that would be less formal. It wouldn't seem so much like a date. Or coffee? I could suggest a cup of coffee down at the deli. That wouldn't be intimidating at all.

He smiled at his errant thoughts. Down one minute and up the next. I'm becoming worse than my moody little ninth graders. No, I'd say worse than that. This is positively pubescent. Emotionally, I'd be placed in the seventh grade.

Thoughts of Agnes led to thoughts of the missing Bible he'd be retrieving. How strange, he thought. I'd just been thinking of reading the Bible when Agnes called.

He was surprised to find that he really did want it back. He had always looked upon it as a sort of failed good luck charm. A talisman that had let him down. A tangible symbol of an uncaring God. After all, how could a Christian die like that? With her Bible right beside her?

He furrowed his brow as he removed a cold ham from

the refrigerator. It didn't seem like such an issue anymore, he told himself. If it had been precious to Linda, he would be glad to have it back.

Her handwriting would be in it, where she had taken notes. Linda had never minded writing in her Bible. He smiled, thinking how horrified he'd been the first time he'd seen her writing in her Bible. She'd laughed her sweet laugh, explaining that it was her handbook, not some collectible to keep under glass. It would be good to see it again.

He sliced himself two thin pieces of ham, then carved up some massive chunks for Teddy. He smiled again as he placed the large gobs of meat in the dog's bowl. "Good thing I don't spoil him."

Wiping his hand on a paper towel, John crossed to the kitchen door and opened it. "Ted, come on. Teddy?"

18

"Teddy?"

John looked with dismay at the empty yard and the open gate. He quickly went down the porch steps and into the yard. In a few strides he was across and standing at the open gate. He looked up and down the street.

"Teddy!" John called and called again, but there was no response. Dumb dog, he thought to himself—no, dumb Renee; she must have left the gate open when she left.

Leaving the yard, John walked the entire block calling for his dog. After a fruitless search, he decided he'd better go get his van and start driving the surrounding streets. He was becoming concerned. Teddy's survival instincts were nonexistent.

John drove slowly down the streets closest to home. He collected a few honks and irritated looks, but he didn't care; he wanted his dog back.

The area churches were starting to let out, adding to the traffic, but John kept driving slowly, calling Teddy's name. He was sure the dog had planned it just this way to make a fool of him.

"Mr. Allan! Hey, Mr. Allan!" John looked up to hear someone calling him. He'd been so busy focusing on the sidewalks he hadn't really paid much attention to the buildings. He saw with a start that he was right across from Linda's old church. He also saw that the long, lanky form of Fred Evans was waving at him from the steps.

John was strongly tempted to just wave and drive on by. But what if Fred had seen his dog? Making a decision, John pulled his van next to the sidewalk and got out.

"Fred," John called out as he crossed the street. "How are you?" he asked as he walked up to him and shook his hand. Before the young man could answer, John was talking again. "I wonder if you've seen my dog? He's run off. He's small. Rather a blond, wheat color. He looks like a shag rug as much as anything."

"No, I'm sorry. We've just got out of church."

"Oh, well. I wouldn't worry, only he's such a stupid animal. He's just a dog, of course, but he's quite helpless." John dug his hands into his pockets. He smiled at Fred for a moment but his eyes drifted away as he compulsively scanned the street.

Fred was touched by the older man's obvious concern for his dog. It didn't mesh with John's aloof personality. "Would you like me to help you look, Mr. Allan? I'm not doing anything this afternoon."

John looked back up at Fred, hesitating. Still, he really wanted to find his dog. His dumb, stupid, aggravating dog.

"I'd really appreciate it, son."

"Just a minute then, while I go inside and tell Mom. We came to church together. You just missed Audrea."

"Oh?" John looked at the double doors with curiosity on his face.

Fred saw the look and was prompted to ask. "Would you like to come in with me?"

John glanced at him and shrugged his shoulders ever so casually. "All right."

As soon as they entered the foyer, John could see that extensive remodeling had been done in the years since his wife had attended. He was impressed at the changes he saw as they entered the small sanctuary. Gray carpet was laid where there had once been a scarred wooden floor. What he had thought of as the world's ugliest pews had been replaced by nice new pews padded with burgundy cloth. Bright brass chandeliers hung from the ceiling instead of the old ball lights. The whole effect was very attractive without being ostentatious. He was impressed.

There were small knots of people scattered about, chatting. John saw as they laughed and joked with each other that they didn't seem to be in any hurry to leave. He caught himself smiling at their good-natured banter.

Fred walked up to a large-framed man who was as tall as he was. As John looked up at the two men he felt like he was in a forest.

"Brother Benning," Fred began, "I want to introduce you to Mr. John Allan, my supervising teacher. Mr. Allan, this is my pastor."

John felt himself tense at the word "pastor." He just wanted to find his dog, forevermore! What was he doing back in this church, meeting the pastor? He forced a tight smile and held out his hand. "Hello," he said in a stiffly neutral tone.

Reverend Victor Benning felt his spiritual radar come on as he looked at the tense man before him. Fred had told him a few things about John. But even if he hadn't, the pastor could sense there was some struggle going on. What's the story here? he asked himself as he extended his hand in a hearty shake. "Hello, Mr. Allan. I'm glad to meet you. Fred speaks very highly of all the help you've given him."

I've given him a hard time, John thought bleakly. But he just nodded his head. "He'll make a fine teacher."

Fred, as usual, blushed. He hastened to turn the subject. "Brother Benning, have you seen my mother? I can't go home. I mean, I can go home, of course, but I was going to help Mr. Allan's dog. I mean, I was going to help him find—"

"Fred?" Reverend Benning interrupted in a kindly tone, as he held up a hand to stop the torrent of words.

"Yes, sir?" Fred asked rather breathlessly.

"She's downstairs in her Sunday school room."

"Good. She'll be right back. No! I mean, I'll be right back."

The two older men watched with amusement as Fred made his quick exit out of the sanctuary. There were two swinging doors at the back. As Fred approached, a small girl ran in, causing the door to swing smartly into Fred's face. A large crack was heard as the door connected with his forehead. He staggered for a moment, then continued on his way.

John winced and shook his head. "That boy has more trouble with doors than anyone I've ever met."

"He's been all bounce and go for as long as I've known him," Reverend Benning said grinning. "But he's all heart."

"And knees and elbows," John added.

The taller man chuckled at that. It was a nice infectious sound that caused John to smile in spite of himself. "His awkward stage has gone on for years now. But there's a depth to that boy that most people don't realize."

John nodded his head in agreement. "Yes, I've seen that side of him."

There was a pause then, as John wished Fred would hurry back. He looked around for a few moments, then commented, "This was a beautiful remodeling job. What a difference from before. I remember there used to be an old 'Frosty Root Beer' clock on that wall."

Surprised, Reverend Benning looked at him. "That awful clock came down the minute I took over the church! That was nearly fourteen years ago. So . . . did you use to attend here?"

152

John was instantly sorry he had said anything. Absently, he twisted the gold ring on his finger. "I came once or twice," he said simply as he looked away.

Reverend Benning could see the shadow stealing across the man's face. He decided a light touch was needed. "Well, I'm glad we've been given a second chance. I'd hate for Frosty Root Beer clocks to be your only impression of our decorating skills! Not to change the subject, but Fred tells me you play basketball?"

"Yes?" John looked up at him puzzled.

"Are you any good?" The blunt question was softened by a warm smile.

John blinked. This was not the question he'd been expecting from a pastor as he stood in the middle of his church. He felt himself relaxing. "Should I be modest or honest?" he asked dryly.

Reverend Benning chuckled again. "Be honest, by all means!"

"I'm pretty good, I guess." John felt a smile tugging at the corner of his mouth.

"I'll tell you why I ask. I've been wanting to get some pick-up games going at the YMCA, but I'm always one or two men short. This is a golfing town, you know."

"True."

"Then what about it? Could you and Fred meet me at the Y someday at noon?"

"Oh, well I suppose someday . . ."

"Great! It's a date. Wednesday, then?"

John felt like he'd missed an important part of the conversation. Somehow he found himself nodding in agreement.

"Yes . . . all right." But after all, it was only basketball.

19

"Wow, I really like your van, Mr. Allan!" Fred enthused as they walked up to the large black and slate gray vehicle. The outside shone from a recent wax job. After they opened the doors and slid into the padded gray seats, he looked around at the plush upholstery, "Is it new?"

John couldn't help but grin at the boy's enthusiasm. He checked his mirrors carefully as he cautiously pulled the big vehicle out into the street.

"No, I've had it for years."

"No kidding, you've sure kept it up nice." Fred trailed his hand across the spotless dashboard. "I'm afraid my car is a little messy."

"Oh?" John tried to sound surprised.

"The guys at church call it the Rolling Waste Dump," Fred admitted sheepishly. "Yeah, I didn't realize it was all that bad until the other day. I found a paper cup from a restaurant that had been out of business for two years."

John chuckled but didn't say anything as he scanned the streets for his dog. Fred followed suit, looking up and down the sidewalks.

Fred couldn't be quiet for too long. After a few

moments, he commented. "As I came in, I heard you talking to Brother Benning about basketball."

"Yes, that's right. He asked if you and I could play at the YMCA on Wednesday."

Fred smiled as he looked out the window, appreciating his pastor's style. Another man might have asked Mr. Allan to the very next church service. Brother Benning must have sensed that that would have alienated Mr. Allan.

"I'd like that. I'll have a lot of free time this week. The college is making arrangements with the Athens County school board for us to student teach there. But that doesn't start until next week."

"It looks like I'll be having a lot of free time too," John commented dryly. "They want us to walk the picket line, though. I'm not too thrilled about that."

"I can imagine."

"I don't even want to think about it. I suppose it might do me some good to go Wednesday. I'll be missing the pick-up games at school."

"Brother Benning will be glad to hear it. I think he loves basketball as much as I do. He went to the same college as my dad. They used to play basketball all the time. That was years before Dad got sick, of course."

"Your dad played too?" John stole a glance at the young man, curious about his father.

"Oh, yeah, I guess he bought me a basketball for my first Christmas. Mom still laughs about it."

John was silent as he thought of a tiny pair of tennis shoes in his dresser at home.

"You're quite a ball player now; your father would have been proud," he said after a few minutes.

"Thanks. I used to really wish he could have lived to see me play, just one game," he shrugged, as he stared down an alleyway. "I don't think about it too much anymore."

"You have a wonderful attitude, Fred. I think it's great you never became angry over your father's death."

John had stopped for a red light. As he checked for traffic he became aware that Fred was staring at him. He turned to look at the young man.

"Mr. Allan, what makes you think I was never angry over my father's death?"

"What?"

"I was angry all right. In fact as I got older and could realize just what I had lost, I was furious. He was my best friend in this world."

"I'm sorry, son," John said with embarrassment. "I guess, I thought . . ."

"That Christians don't get angry?" Fred finished gently.

John concentrated on pulling the van into the intersection, not sure of what to say.

"Believe me, I was angry enough for two people. When I was in my early teens, I was a handful. I'm afraid I gave Mom a hard time." Fred looked away from John, towards the street. "Every time she'd tell me what a great Christian Dad had been, my stomach would tie up into little knots."

"You couldn't understand why God would let such a good Christian die?" John asked quietly.

"Exactly. I mean it wasn't like Dad had been some awful, hardened sinner. The last thing I'd hear at night was him praying for me. Even when he became so sick that I'd have to go to his room to say good night, he'd be praying for me, for Mom, for everyone, really."

"You don't seem angry or bitter now."

"I'm not. Mom helped a lot. She told me if I was angry, I was angry. But that I shouldn't forget God knew exactly what I was feeling, so I'd better tell Him all about it."

"That kind of scared me at first. I mean, how do you tell the Creator of the universe that you're mad at Him? But like Mom said, He already knew it."

John found himself gripping the steering wheel tighter, his own stomach in knots. "By simply telling God you were angry, you worked through it?" he asked skeptically.

157

Fred shook his head. "Oh no, it took more than that. But what Mom knew was that by telling the Lord about my feelings, no matter how negative they were, I was at least talking to Him. Strange as it may seem, I was praying. God could work with that."

John frowned, thinking over what the young man was saying. John had always thought of God as a force or a power. Fred talked about God as if He were a person. As if He were a friend.

"You and God seem to be on pretty good terms now." There was no sarcasm in his voice but rather a mild wistfulness.

"We are," Fred answered catching his tone. "Because I kept those lines of communication open, He was able to show me that He grieved with me. That He felt what I felt. Do you know what the shortest verse in the Bible is?"

"No."

"'Jesus wept.'"

"He cried?"

"That's right. His friend Lazarus had died. The Lord cried, Mr. Allan. Even though He knew He was going to raise him from the dead. The Lord used that portion of Scripture to comfort me. He showed me that even though He knew my dad would be in the resurrection, would live forever, He grieved with me right now."

"But . . . Fred, why grieve at all? Since He's so all powerful, why did she die?"

She? Fred was confused for a moment at John's unconscious slip. Then he realized what the man was really asking. He shrugged. "I don't know."

"You don't know?" John fought against irritation. He had thought the young man would have some answers for him. "If you don't know why she . . . I mean, he died, then how do you . . . believe? How do you believe in a just, merciful God when such cosmic injustice has ruined your life?"

Several very good verses of Scripture came to Fred's

lips, but he felt a sudden check in his spirit. "Do you like to do research, Mr. Allan?"

"What?" John snapped. Despite himself, he was angry now.

"Well . . . when you want your students to learn something and have them keep it in their long-term memory, don't you make them look up the information for themselves? Have them do the research?"

John stared rather sullenly out the window, as Fred wondered if he were totally blowing his first chance to help this man. "Your point, Fred?"

"Mr. Allan, I could give you some pat little answers about trust and faith. I could even quote you some great verses of Scripture. But I think what you truly need to do is go to the source. Tell God what you're feeling. Ask questions. Do the research."

John sat up ramrod straight, his face a blank mask. "I thought we were talking about your father," he said coldly.

"I thought we were too, Mr. Allan, . . . at first."

John tried to remind himself that it wasn't Fred he was angry with. But it took him several long minutes of silence to regain his composure. "Son," he began in a more normal tone. "I know you mean well."

Fred bit his lip in frustration, wondering how much damage he had done. He wished fervently for the right words that could make everything clear to the unhappy man beside him. His brain was stuck in neutral.

After driving down a few more streets without any sign of the dog, John finally spoke. "I do appreciate your helping me look for Ted. Unfortunately, we're not having any luck here. Can I drive you home?"

Fred looked sadly out the window, certain he had spoiled everything. "The church is closer. We'll be having choir practice soon, if you want to drop me off there."

"Sure."

They drove the rest of the way in silence.

Why does that nice young man always bring out the worst in me? John asked himself as he watched Fred trudge up the steps of the church. He lingered for a moment, toying with the idea of apologizing.

As he sat in his van, he began to hear the strains of music coming from the church. He rolled his window down to catch the sound. Several windows in the old church building had been left open and he could clearly hear the strong young voices.

"There are loved ones in the glory, whose dear forms you often miss. When you close your earthly story, will you join them in their bliss?"

John stared at the steering wheel, struck by the words. He wanted to pull away, to leave the song and the little church far behind him. He couldn't move. He sat like a rock as each word, as each line, reached out to him.

"One by one their seats were emptied. One by one they went away. Now the family is parted. Will it be complete one day?"

John took a deep shuddering breath as he gripped the steering wheel and pulled out into the street.

John's already heavy heart sank a little further as he pulled his van in front of his empty yard. He had left the gate open, hoping Teddy would return and be waiting for him on the porch. It was very strange to turn the lock in his front door and not hear his little dog scratching on the other side, waiting to jump up in greeting.

"Dumb, stupid dog," John mumbled as he walked by the two dog dishes near the kitchen doorway.

Without stopping to remove his jacket, he went straight to his old computer that he kept in a small side room. In moments he was composing a notice for the Lost and Found section of the newspaper. He planned to take it there first thing in the morning.

As the notice came through on his printer, he sat back in his chair and looked sadly around the room. This room had been set aside for the nursery. Its walls were the same bright yellow. Their cheery color mocked him now.

"Enough!" he said aloud. "This is enough!"

He switched the printer off and shut down the computer. He pushed back his chair, then sat very still. He wondered if he should clasp his hands. He knew he couldn't make himself kneel.

Instead he placed his hands on his knees and shut his eyes. He was quiet for a moment, feeling rather foolish. Yet he was becoming desperate. He wanted to be free of his sadness, to have his "days of mourning ended."

"All right," he whispered. "I'm told You already know what I'm feeling." That does make sense, he told himself. Being God would entail being all knowing. "Then You know how angry I've been. How lonely. I don't know if that matters to You or not." John was quiet for a while, gathering his thoughts. "But she mattered to You, didn't she? She loved You, surely You knew that, You're God!" John's voice rose ever so slightly, but he was keeping his emotions firmly in check.

"I've lost everything, but I'm not complaining to You about that. After all, I never followed You. Why should You look after me?" A lone tear slipped down his face. "But her . . . it's not right. It's just not right."

John put his face in his hands. Peace did not come flooding into his soul. Clouds of joy did not sweep him away. Yet he could not shake the feeling that all the time he had been talking, Someone had been listening.

He slowly rose from his chair and walked back out to the porch. He sank into a wicker chair, glad for the soft, yielding cushions. He suddenly felt very tired. As he leaned his head back to watch the setting sun, he could hear the tolling of the church bells in the distance, calling people to the evening service.

What a long Sunday it had been!

20

The next morning John was not awakened by a cold, wet nose in his ear. His eyes flew open at the angry sound of his electric alarm clock. Without stopping to put on his robe, he flung his covers back and got out of bed. In a few long strides he was in the kitchen. When he opened the back door, the only thing he saw on the porch was the morning newspaper.

His eyes scanned the yard, making sure the gate was still open.

"Stupid, stupid dog," he said as he picked up the paper and returned to the kitchen. He looked at the refrigerator for a moment, but he really didn't feel like eating. If he hurried, he reasoned, he could drop his notice off at the newspaper before he had to be on the picket line.

John returned to his bedroom to get ready for the day. As he made his preparations, he remembered there'd be one bright spot today. He'd be seeing Agnes again. The thought brought a smile to his face. Maybe he would ask her to go to dinner with him after all.

"You are a crazy old man," he sternly told his reflection in the mirror. Then patting his still flat stomach, he amended, "Well, a crazy middle-aged man, then."

163

His eyes strayed to the silver-framed picture of Linda on his dresser. He felt a small pang of guilt. After all, he was meeting Agnes to retrieve Linda's Bible. As he picked up the familiar picture, he thought her bright smile seemed even more compassionate than usual. No, Linda would have understood.

He put the picture down gently and left to face the day.

When John arrived at the little building that housed Glendale's only newspaper, he saw it was not only open but full of activity.

The *Glendale Times* didn't have it easy. There wasn't that much news in a town the size of Glendale. The national wire services and local club news were the main sources of news, just barely padding the paper to nine or ten pages. When the *Times* did get a story of interest, the staff tended to worry it to death. They would stretch some of the slimmest items to the breaking point.

John smiled, remembering when the newspaper had devoted the front page to the Glendale Tree Commission and their "Valiant Fight Against Dutch Elm Disease." There had been interviews of "experts" and a large ugly photo of a rotting tree limb.

As he pushed back the heavy steel and plexiglass door, he had to step aside to let a small knot of two reporters and a photographer through. They were trailed by a tall, skinny man who wore his dark hair pulled back into a sleek ponytail. A ponytail John mused, right here in River City!

The man with the ponytail was giving last-minute instructions to the news crew. "Now remember, guys, I want lots of pictures. Especially faces. Get me the kids' reactions as they step off the school buses." He held up his hands as if making a frame. "I really want at least one shot of a kid looking at a teacher holding a picket sign. Take several snaps and I'll put the best one on the front page."

He pointed a long, skinny finger at a pretty black woman. "Cindy, find the emotional ones, the angry ones. If the kid or the teacher isn't frowning, don't interview them. Get the emotion, see if you can't find a crank, for a color piece." He then turned to a rather bored-looking young man who was smoking. "Jared, you talk to the teachers crossing the picket line. Ask 'em how they feel about being on the other side."

"You mean the scabs?" he said with a sneer as he flicked the cigarette into the bushes.

"Now, now, we want to be objective, Jared," the man admonished, placing his hands on his thin hips. Then a slow smile lifted his lips. "But bandy that word around; you'll get a better interview."

The crew found that amusing, showing rather wolfish smiles all around. The pack is ready for the hunt, John thought miserably. He had stood chained to the open door, listening to the whole exchange. He let the door shut and walked inside, hoping that the news crew would be done by the time he got to the school.

The front office of the *Glendale Times* was laid out very nicely. The carpeting was deep and plush enough that footprints could be seen in its velvety green nap. Plants lined the cream and sea-foam walls. To the right a receptionist sat at a bronze- and glass-trimmed desk. To the far left of the large room a bronze-trimmed counter separated a bank of clerks from the reception area.

The advertisers must pay well, John thought as he walked up to the receptionist.

"May I help you?" the woman asked pleasantly. She was an extremely attractive woman. Her dark chocolate-colored skin was highlighted by the burgundy sweater she wore. Her intelligent brown eyes were also very pretty.

It struck John that the newspaper was going to some lengths to present a good first impression. It was a shame some of that effort hadn't carried over to the paper itself.

"Yes, ma'am. I'd like to place an ad in the Lost and Found section of the paper."

She smiled and pointed to the counter behind him. "See that woman over there? She's in charge of that department."

John thanked her and walked across the room towards the woman the receptionist had indicated.

The young woman behind the counter seemed vaguely familiar, but John couldn't place her. She was bent over a computer terminal, frowning distractedly. When she looked up at the sound of John's approach, her face broke into a smile of pure sunshine. "Mr. Allan! How are you?"

John smiled warmly, trying to place her. He'd had so many students over the years, surely he'd had her at some time in one of his classes. He reached across the counter to give her a handshake, while he silently begged his memory to come up with a name. "Hello yourself! It's good to see you again." Who is this girl? Why don't they give these people name tags? he asked himself, not hearing the footsteps coming up behind him.

"You know, Mr. Allan, you were always my favorite teacher. I got into journalism because of your English classes."

Before John could respond he felt a hand on his shoulder. Turning, he found himself looking up into the face of the skinny man with the ponytail.

"So you're a teacher, eh? I'm sorry my reporters missed you." He gave John a large smile that didn't reach the man's ice blue eyes. "I'm Glen Hatfield, the editor here."

"Hello," John said simply.

"I'm surprised you're not on the picket lines, Mr. Albert, or maybe you don't believe in the strike?" Still smiling, he pinned John with a cold stare.

"Actually, I . . ."

"Tell you what, Mr. Alvin, I bet you're pretty disgusted with the whole situation. I mean, don't you think the town is taking you and your colleagues for granted?"

"I'm not—"

"Or maybe you're one of those people who don't believe in public servants going on strike."

"Well, I—"

"Then again," Hatfield's eyes narrowed into little thin slits, "Maybe you just want to play it smart. You won't go on strike, but you'll reap all the benefits the union comes up with."

"Now, just a minute—"

"I want to hear your opinions, but I really want you to talk to my reporters." He reached into a pocket of his designer jeans and took out a business card. "Here," he said handing the card to John. "Are you going by the school this morning?"

John nodded slowly.

"Great! Hand this to one of my reporters. Tell them we had a long talk, and I want them to interview you." He gave John a rather smarmy wink. "You'd like that, wouldn't you?"

"As a matter of fact—"

"Good, good. There you go, Mr. Albert, give them that card and tell them what you think!" He gave John a nod, then glanced at the girl behind the counter. "Don't you have enough to do, Tina?" he asked sternly.

"Tina was trying to help me place a notice," John said, finally finishing a sentence.

Hatfield cocked an eyebrow. "Of course," he muttered. Then giving them both a dismissive nod, he strode out of the room.

"Thanks, Mr. Allan," the girl whispered. "He's a wonderful editor. He's just very . . . intense."

"No doubt, Tina," John said gladly, emphasizing her name. "Tina, could I get you to place this ad for my missing dog?" He handed her his notice, wondering why she was looking at him so strangely.

"Sure, Mr. Allan," the girl said, an odd note in her voice.

"Thanks, Tina," he smiled again. "It was good to see you again, Tina." He walked out, oblivious to the rather sour farewell she gave him.

After John had left, the girl turned to the man working at the terminal beside her. "Sam, first my boss, now Mr. Allan. Why is everyone calling me Tina?"

The man looked up from his computer and shrugged. "Beats me, Terry."

21

His stomach was slowly churning as John drove towards the school. He didn't want to be on the picket line. He didn't want his students to see him in that way. He really didn't know how he felt about the strike at all.

The union had some very valid points. The school district was facing a $600,000-deficit by the end of the fiscal year. The failed levy would have raised $1.1 million for four years. Now, how could the school board cut $600,000 from a budget that was already suffering? The union was afraid, and rightly so, that those enormous cuts would come from teacher salaries or even teacher layoffs.

By careful budgeting, John had always managed on his salary, but he was just one man. He knew it was hard for all the teachers with families. He knew several divorced female teachers who had children to support. They often sold cosmetics or other items on the side to make ends meet. In fact, he couldn't think of one male teacher whose wife didn't work outside the home. No, the only teachers who didn't have to supplement their income were single like himself or had a working spouse. He thought of Steve and his wife, Carol. She had wanted to stay home with her small children, but she spent most evenings as a cashier at a grocery store. He really could understand Steve not striking, even if he wasn't sure he agreed with him. Ironically, as a coach and physical education teacher, Steve's job was in more jeopardy than most teachers walking the picket line.

John sighed loudly. Many factories in the area had cut back or even shut down entirely. As he'd said a hundred times, how can you get people to vote for more taxes in a depressed economy?

The question that John seldom heard addressed was, What about the school boards themselves? In many states there was only one board per county, but not here. In this county there were four school boards alone. That meant four superintendents, each with one or two assistants, not to mention their own set of staff, their own buildings and offices to run. Wasn't it all too top heavy? Was it really cost effective? He shook his head. No one seemed to mind all that.

His internal dialogue dried up as he saw the long, grim line of teachers in front of the school. There would be no parking in the parking lot today. A row of male teachers were already guarding its entrance. Surely, they wouldn't try to stop the buses, John reasoned, concerned. Someone could get hurt.

John parked his van a good distance down the street, then walked slowly up the sidewalk. He wore his tweed cap pulled down low, with the collar of his khaki windjammer pushed up, wishing he could become invisible. The art teacher, Hal Mendoza, fell into step beside him. He too, wore his hat low and slouched down. Of course, since the man topped out at six feet five inches, his chances of being inconspicuous were quite a bit slimmer than John's. He grinned at John sheepishly.

"Maybe we should have just worn white sheets and burned an effigy of the dollar sign," he commented.

"Or maybe called in some substitute teachers to strike for us?" John asked, matching his tone.

"Substitute strikers? Now there's an idea."

As they approached the school with its line of teachers, John noticed Calvin Loring and Renee Grayson were bustling up and down the sidewalk handing out signs and placards. Even in the crisp fall air of early morning, Calvin was in shirt sleeves, two dark rings of sweat already forming under his armpits. Renee was wearing another one of her impossible outfits. She had on a long, striped poncho with a bright purple scarf for a headband. John thought her silver-trimmed, purple-leather boots gave her an "Elvis does Vegas" look.

John had been staring at Calvin and Renee in bemused distaste when Mendoza took his long arm and quickly pulled John into line. "Stand back, or Loring will give us one of his stupid signs."

"Right," John agreed. "He probably stayed up all night printing them out on his beloved computer." He couldn't take his eyes off Renee's boots. "Say, where do you suppose you get purple leather?"

Mendoza shook his head. "I never saw a purple cow," he said with a straight face.

John smiled and looked at his watch. He sobered as he saw the time. "The buses will be coming soon."

"I hate this," Mendoza mumbled.

"Oh, no," John said softly, as he saw a familiar car pulling up the street. It was Steve.

Brooks's little red Chevette managed to look vulnerable as it made its way towards the parking lot. The jaunty and comical bumper stickers plastered all over its rear hatch seemed sadly out of place as it drove towards the stone-faced teachers blocking the entrance. John held his breath. Steve had worked among these men for years; surely no one would harass him. Would they?

One of the men towards the very center of the entrance looked over at Loring, while the little car and its anxious driver waited.

171

John could see that one of its brake lights were out. He could also see that Steve's face was set in a blank stare, looking straight ahead.

Calvin looked disgusted, but he only shook his head angrily. The men in the line took their cue from him and began to back away from the entrance with a tantalizing slowness.

John let out his breath in a quiet rush.

"Who put Calvin in charge?" Mendoza grumbled in his deep baritone, as he thoughtfully stroked his gray-streaked beard.

John looked up at him, unsure. Was he just irritated at Calvin, or did he think Steve got off too easy? He wanted Steve to be able to have a normal life when this was all over.

A low rumbling was coming from down the street. The buses. John tried to look resolutely straight ahead, to detach himself from the whole episode, but he couldn't. As he heard the buses coming nearer, he slowly turned his head towards them.

He was immediately sorry. For there, in front of the first bus, was a police car. A police car!

"Does someone think that we'd hurt these young people?" he blurted out.

"Apparently," Mendoza answered, equally annoyed.

The cruiser stopped in the middle of the street, directly across from John's section of the picket line. Two officers got out of the car. The driver started towards the school, while his partner stayed in the street to direct traffic and man the school's crosswalk.

The first officer, a young man with bright red hair, seemed to be approaching John and Mendoza when Calvin and Renee came up, demanding his attention.

"Officer, officer!" Calvin said panting for breath. "What is this? We have every legal right in the world to be here."

172

The policeman turned his gaze towards Calvin. The young man wasn't much taller than John, though he looked as if he spent all his off hours lifting weights. Lots of weights. Big heavy weights.

"This is a legal assembly," Calvin continued. "Striking is still allowed in this country."

The policeman only looked at Calvin, though John noticed a tight cord of muscle seemed to be coming out on his neck.

"Would you two gentlemen step aside, please?" he asked John and Mendoza in a polite, quiet voice that bordered on a whisper.

"Step . . . step aside!" Calvin thundered. "Now you see here, young man . . ."

A tiny vein along the young man's temple seemed more pronounced as he turned back to Calvin. "The students will need to come through here to get into the school," he said in the same low tones. Without changing his bland expression, he nodded to John and Mendoza who had obediently complied. Then he walked back to the buses.

"Well, I guess he knows he can't push us around," Calvin blustered. "The idea! Bringing police here!"

"That's right, Calvin. I'm glad you were here to speak up for us," Renee said, pointedly ignoring John.

But John wasn't paying any attention. With the rest of the teachers, he watched in silence as the policeman motioned the first bus to open its doors. It was full of adults, substitute teachers from other counties, and a handful of teachers from Glendale High who had chosen not to strike.

"Cowards," Calvin said loudly to Renee. "At least Brooks had the guts to face the music on his own."

Calvin, Renee and a few other striking teachers glared as the busload filed past into the school. Most of the striking teachers were of the same mind as John, not hating

173

these people but hating the events that had brought them.

Calvin had turned to make some crack to John, when he noticed he wasn't carrying a picket sign. "Here, John, you'll want one of these," he said as he pulled out a large sign he had tucked under his sweaty armpit. He abruptly thrust it into John's hands.

"Calvin, really . . ." John began, disgusted. As he held the sign up, looking for a dry place to hold it, he heard the quiet voice of the policeman behind him.

"Excuse us, mister, we're coming through."

John turned back and to his left, to see the policeman leading a group of students. John found himself looking into the dismayed face of Audrea Givens, who had stopped to stare at the sign he held. Just as the policeman lightly touched her arm to get her moving again, a bright flash of white light momentarily blinded them all.

When the little group had regained their sight, they saw the photographer from the *Glendale Times* smiling at them. The photographer, a chunky young man still fighting acne, turned to the two reporters beside him.

"Man, what a shot! What a shot! Police guarding students from irate teacher!" he enthused.

"Kid, that one will make the wires," the reporter called Cindy said knowingly.

"Gee, do you really think so?"

"Count on it," the other reporter, Jared, said in his usual bored fashion. "It'll be all over the country by tomorrow."

John stared in horror at the photographer, then looked down at his sign, only to receive a fresh shock.

"NO LEVY, NO LARNING!"

"It's . . . it's not even spelled right!" he gasped at Calvin.

"Oh." Calvin at least had the grace to look embarrassed for a moment. Then he shrugged. "Sorry, I was up all night. That was the last one I made."

John threw the sign to the pavement and strode over to the photographer. "Now see here. You can't use that photograph! It's misleading."

The photographer clutched his camera protectively, then looked at the two reporters for support. Before the woman could speak, the male reporter stepped forward. "You feel pretty strongly about this, don't you?" he asked smoothly. In one fluid motion he managed to light a fresh cigarette and surreptitiously start the small recorder he was holding.

"Well, of course I do! It puts me in a terrible position."

"I see," Jared said nodding. "You think you're unfairly represented? Mr. . . . ?"

"Allan, John Allan," he answered flustered. "That's right. What will people think when they see it?"

"That you're a frustrated professional that's been pushed to the breaking point by the public's indifference?"

"Right. I mean . . . I am frustrated, but . . ." John paused, feeling he was losing the point of the conversation. "I would never want people to think . . ."

"That after devoting your whole life to education you'll be denied a viable income?"

"Well, a man has to live, but . . ."

"You're tired of empty promises that evaporate when the public has to pay the bills?" Jared took a long, satisfying draw on his cigarette.

"Yes, but what about the photograph?" John demanded. "I don't want it in the newspaper!"

Jared blew a long puff of smoke over the shorter man's head.

"Oh, the photo?" he asked lazily. "I don't have anything to do with that. You'll have to ask the photographer."

"For heaven's sake!" John growled as he moved past the reporter. But as he looked up the sidewalk, he saw the

175

photographer along with the woman reporter, was gone.

John snapped an angry glance at the remaining reporter, but he only shrugged and took another drag on his cigarette.

Before John could say anything, the man turned and began interviewing Renee and Calvin. They were only too pleased to offer up their opinions for print.

Disgusted, John shoved his hands in his pockets and strode down the sidewalk towards his van.

22

Okay, let's see if I have this all straight, John thought dismally to himself as he pulled the van away from the curb. My best friend isn't speaking to me, I'm out of work, on strike, and my dog's run away. It sounds like a really bad country and western song. Not to mention poor Clark, or Renee, or the fact that I will probably be on the front page tomorrow looking like some fire-breathing rabble-rouser.

As he entered the next street, he realized he had nowhere to go. It seemed so odd to be out and about on a school day. He felt a wave of depression threatening to break over him. He didn't want to give into it.

"I know . . ." he murmured to himself as he turned a corner and headed for the Goodwill Store.

A few streets later, John was pulling into the Goodwill parking lot. The store itself was rather sad looking and run down, but it boasted a wonderful location that had many a real estate agent licking their lips in hopeful anticipation.

Its front faced another street in the small Glendale business district, but its back door opened onto a wonderful old cobbled lane that lined the shores of the Ohio River. As the years had gone by, a beautiful river-front park had been developed and several quaint shops and cafes facing the river had been built on either side of the sagging Goodwill building.

After parking the van, John paused a moment and looked across the parking lot to the river. It was beautiful. He leaned back in his seat and took a deep breath. Dinner? Never. She'd never go to dinner with a man she'd just met in the store. He looked in the rear-view mirror at a pair of worried hazel eyes. Coffee? Next door at the deli? He'd be sure and tell her he was a schoolteacher. People always tended to trust teachers.

He nodded to himself and reached out to take the door handle. Oh, no! The photograph! He suddenly thought of that awful news photo. What would she think of him if she saw it? He sank back into his seat, miserable.

No, he told himself. I'll explain what happened. She'll probably laugh about it. She has such a nice laugh. After a few more moments of this internal pep talk, John left the van and entered the shop.

He looked expectantly at the counter, but an elderly lady was there instead of Agnes. The tiny woman was rather birdlike, with a chubby little body and thin arms and legs. A kind smile lit her face.

"Hello," she said in a high, quivering voice. "May I help you?"

"Yes, ma'am," John said kindly. "Is Agnes working today? She was keeping something for me."

The woman blinked a few times as if trying to remember something. "Are you Mr. Allan?"

"Yes, ma'am."

The woman smiled at him cheerfully, as if that settled everything.

John waited a few moments, then gently prompted her. "Sooo . . . is Agnes here?"

"Oh. No, but she left a message." The woman smiled pleasantly again.

"And the message?"

She blinked rapidly a few times, tilting her head to one side. She opened her mouth after a moment, then closed it uncertainly. Finally she said with dismay, "Oh, dear. I'm afraid I've forgotten!"

"That's all right," he said trying to hide his disappointment. "I can come back tomorrow."

"Well, all right then. I really am sorry."

The little woman looked so mournful that John patted her hand. "Don't worry about it!" he said briskly, then turned to leave. He had set the little bell over the door ringing when she called out to him.

"Oh, wait." She came around the counter with surprising agility, a small package in her hands. "I do remember I was to give you this."

"The Bible," John smiled, taking the package from her.

She beamed at him, clasping her thin arms across her chunky little body. "Ohh, is that what it is? Well, there's a world of comfort in that Book, son."

John was warmed by her smile. It had been a good two decades since anyone had called him son. He also noticed her vagueness seemed to melt away as she spoke on her favorite subject. It was rather charming.

"'O the depth of the riches both of the wisdom and knowledge of God! How unsearchable are his judgments, and his ways past finding out!'" A fire had lit in her eyes that touched John to his core. The words she spoke seemed to transform her.

"A quotation?" he asked humbly.

"Oh, yes. Romans 11:3," she answered firmly, then chuckled. "Somedays, I can hardly remember anything. But the Scripture," she tapped her temple with a gnarled finger, "the Scripture has never left me."

"That must be a real comfort to you."

The little woman looked at him shrewdly, her eyes

suddenly piercing. John dropped his gaze for a moment; his words had sounded hollow and placating in his own ears.

"The Scriptures can be a real comfort to anyone," she returned. She patted the package he now held. "You have any questions, son? You'll find your answers in there."

He had thought to mouth another polite response. Instead he surprised himself by asking honestly, "Will I?"

"Ask, and it shall be given you; seek, and ye shall find; knock, and it shall be opened unto you."

"Another quote?" he asked gently.

She smiled a smile of purest sunshine. A joy lit her frail frame that was almost palpable. "Matthew 7:7. I could quote you hundreds, but maybe you need to read this for yourself."

How closely her words echoed Fred's advice of doing his own research. John nodded at her slowly, a gentle resignation creeping into his soul. "Yes, maybe I should. Everything seems to be pointing that way," he said, patting the brown paper of the package.

"Ah . . . Has the good Lord been trying to get your attention?"

John looked at her in surprise. Now there was a thought! "Well, I don't know about that . . . but life has been rather trying lately. Still . . ." he struggled to regain a lighter tone. "Besides, I'm sure God isn't too concerned with someone like me."

"'But God commendeth his love toward us, in that, while we were yet sinners, Christ died for us.' Romans 5:8."

John looked longingly at the door. He couldn't believe this woman would be talking to him like this. You didn't talk religion with strangers. You certainly didn't speak about Christ dying on the cross!

The little woman seemed to read his very thoughts. "You'll have to forgive my bluntness, dear. It's a privilege of old age. I don't have many years left, so I don't waste time on small talk."

He only smiled at her as he gratefully went out the door.

"'Draw nigh to God, and he will draw nigh to you.' James 4:8!" she called out cheerfully as he left the shop.

John didn't slow down until he got to his van. His hand was on the handle when he looked out towards the river front. He again thought of how lovely it was. Looking back over his shoulder to make sure the little Christian lady wasn't following, he decided to walk down to the park.

He laughed to himself, Surely I'm not afraid of that sweet little old lady? He knew it wasn't the lady but the words she spoke, such powerful words that weren't her own. He looked down thoughtfully at the small package he carried.

As John approached the shore he saw a large flock of Canadian geese bobbing on the water. He smiled in appreciation. He sat down on a well-worn park bench to watch the geese.

Despite his quietness, the geese became edgy and in a few moments took to the sky. It was a lovely sight that cheered him. They made a nearly perfect V formation as they flew down river.

He knew all about the aerodynamic benefits of the flock flying in formation. But how in the world did the geese know? It struck John forcibly for the first time.

If there was such a design, such a plan in nature, someone had to have planned it. And if someone went to so much trouble to plan for these geese . . . John let the thought trail off as he gently began to unwrap the Bible.

As he tore the paper away, he saw again the cross-stitched cover Linda had made for it. When he opened it, he saw again her elegant handwriting making notes on nearly every page.

A yellowed piece of paper fluttered from the Bible and fell into his lap. He gently picked it up and read the words "Prayer List." He saw that his own name was at the top of the list.

"Oh, Linda did I make you unhappy?" he murmured. He thought of all the times Linda had had to go to church alone. He remembered all the times she would come home from church, eager to share it with him, only to have him brush it aside. She had never complained, but now for the first time he realized how disappointed she must have been. She had asked so little of him. Why couldn't he have gone to church to please her?

It would have pleased her to know that he had her Bible now and did want to read it. Only where did one start? As he flipped through the pages, he felt slightly overwhelmed. A verse seemed to suddenly leap out at him.

"The fool hath said in his heart, There is no God. Corrupt are they, and have done abominable iniquity: there is none that doeth good." Psalm 53:1.

He blinked at the forcefulness of it. A fool? Abominable iniquity? He certainly didn't like to think of himself in those terms. And what had that little old lady said about sinners?

John had to admit that he had thought of himself as something of a victim for so long he hated to think in terms of his own responsibility.

He looked up again to see the flock of geese in the distance, fading from view. A plan. Was there a plan for his life? If there was, what could he do about it?

23

All of his life John had lived by one credo: "Knowledge is power." Education and learning were his meat and drink. When he was a scrawny teenager, too short to make the basketball team, he had spent an entire summer learning the sport. The following school year he had become so skillful that the coach had ignored his height and put him on the first string. When his family was too poor to send him to college, his high grades and academic achievements had earned him enough scholarships to go to one of the finest universities in the state. He firmly believed anyone could master anything if he just had the right knowledge.

That night as he sat alone in his living room, Linda's Bible in his hand, he made a vow. If there was a God, if there was any sort of plan in the chaos of his life, he would have that knowledge. He couldn't go through the rest of his life ignorant of what Linda had held dear. Then after he had made a careful study of the Bible, he could come to some sort of decision. A sane, emotionless decision based on the intellectual honesty he had always lived by. After fifteen years of denial, he was ready to come to grips with the spiritual dimension of life.

He slowly opened the Bible, not really sure how to study it other than to just begin reading. It occurred to him that Linda had often said a small prayer each night before reading her Bible. That might be in order now. He bent his head and shut his eyes.

"All right, God, I'm not going to get all emotional about this." He stopped, thinking there was no need to sound antagonistic. "I mean, I've been so upset for weeks now, I need to be rational and logical in my approach here. I guess I'm trying to say . . . if You're interested . . . I'd like to know more."

Despite his resolve to remain emotionless, John felt something welling up in his heart, making his voice thick.

"I'm . . . alone. It would be nice to know that the words I'm speaking are being heard . . . by someone. I guess if I could learn that there was a reason behind everything . . . a reason why wonderful people die young . . . I wouldn't even have to know what the specifics were, just that there were reasons. Only to know that there's some purpose, some plan."

John opened his eyes to stare at the page before him.

"I've lost everything I've ever cared about," he said calmly. Then he shyly looked up at the ceiling. "But You know, I've even seemed to have lost some of my anger."

In his own scholarly fashion, John began to read the Book of Genesis. He read of love won and lost. He read of civilizations built and then washed away. He read of unspeakable tragedies caused by man's willfulness and glorious victories wrested by a loving God.

Near midnight, John came to the story of Joseph. He read with fascination of a young man who lost everything not once but twice. As he neared the end of Joseph's story he saw the purpose of it all. Joseph had suffered terribly, but thousands of lives had been saved. Even Joseph's suffering came to an end as the young man achieved a position of great wealth and stature. There had been a plan.

Through the fifty chapters of Genesis there had been a plan. Through the hundreds of years, through countless lives, there had always been a plan.

As John prepared for bed that night he placed the Bible in front of Linda's picture. He stared at the picture. She would always be young and beautiful. She would never know forty as he knew it now. She would never feel her body slowing down. The ravages of lingering diseases would never touch her. It struck him that whatever tragedy had gone before, Linda was safe now. Feeling better than he had for a long, long time, John went to sleep.

He awoke early the next morning to a car door slamming shut, then the sound of a muffled yelp. He lay in bed for a moment in groggy confusion until he heard knocking on the front door punctuated by the sound of barking.

"Teddy!" he exclaimed jumping from the bed and grabbing his bathrobe. He was at his front door in moments, pulling it open.

A blur of wheat-colored fur jumped into his arms, knocking him off balance. He didn't have a good grasp on the dog, so instead of risking dropping him, John sank to the kitchen floor in happy confusion, totally unmindful of his usual dignity.

"Teddy! You idiot, you fool! You stupid, stupid dog!" he said lovingly as the dog licked his face in ecstasy.

"Well, if I'd known you felt like that, I'd have just kept him. My kids love him," a familiar voice spoke from the doorway.

"Steve!" John said with surprise as he saw his friend towering over him.

Steve nodded ruefully, a little awkward despite his humor. "Yeah, but quit groveling; you may stand in my presence."

"Oh hush, and help me up. Teddy has me pinned."

Steve reached down and helped John up, but John didn't let go of his hand. Rather, he grasped it firmly. "It's good to see you, Steve."

Surprised by his warm affection, Steve couldn't think of a ready quip. He only shook John's hand in return.

Teddy was not ready to share the limelight. He jumped up, begging to be held. John readily complied.

"You dumb dog. Couldn't find your way out of a paper bag. I don't know why I was worried; you're not smart enough to get into trouble."

Teddy just licked his face in happy agreement. John looked up at Steve. "Thank you. He's just an old hairball, but I kinda like him."

"Kinda? You old softy, that's not good grammar. You must have been worried sick. I found him moping around my neighborhood last night. He must have gotten lost and couldn't get back home. I would have called you, only it was so late."

"Come on in, Steve; have a seat. Let Teddy and I get this reunion over with, then I can fix us something. You haven't had breakfast yet, surely?"

Steve settled into the recliner, while John kept Teddy beside him on the couch. Steve was tickled at the sight of his normally calm, immaculate friend. John's bathrobe was all rumpled, and he had wisps of hair sticking out over his ears. He hugged the dog to himself, like a little boy who'd recovered a lost toy.

"He means a lot to you, doesn't he?" Steve asked softly.

John looked up at him, considering his answer. "When Linda died, I swore I'd never get close to anyone again. I figured I could totally control my emotions. So if I controlled my emotions I could control my pain." He shook his head. "I was wrong. You have to love, even if it takes the form of loving a roomful of students or a little dog." He paused for a moment, then he looked Steve in the eye. "Even if that love takes the form of friendship with some overgrown jock of a gym teacher."

"Or some underdeveloped, uppity English teacher."

"Even so."

"Say, are we having a serious conversation?" Steve asked with mock concern.

"Don't worry, it's over."

"Whew, that's good. Did someone say something about breakfast?"

"I believe they did," John said as he rose from the couch.

"Well, you be sure and wash your hands now. I don't want dog hairs in my eggs," Steve said as he relaxed back into the recliner.

"I'll have you know, Teddy doesn't shed!" John called from the kitchen.

"Oh? Well, I took one look at his owner and I figured it was a family thing," Steve yelled back.

"Ho, ho, ho. Make yourself useful and bring in the newspaper, will you? It should be on the back porch."

"Yeah, yeah," Steve grumbled good-naturedly as he unfolded himself from the comfortable chair. He stopped a moment in the kitchen doorway, looking awkward again. "Say, I don't have to apologize or anything? Admit that I've been acting like a real jerk?"

John never looked up from the eggs he was cracking into the frying pan. "No, you don't have to apologize. As for acting like a jerk? I never suspected for a minute that you were acting."

"Yeah, well . . . hey!"

"Just get the paper, Steve."

Steve obediently fetched the paper and returned to the kitchen. A look of purest wonder filled his face as he gazed at the front page.

"Uh, John?"

John, busy getting plates from a cabinet didn't turn around. "Yes?"

"How do you spell 'learning'?"

John spun around in horror, nearly dropping the two plates he held. He threw them on the table and snatched the newspaper from his friend's hand. "Oh no, oh no, oh no," he moaned as he stared at his full-color, half-page picture. There he was, holding the misspelled sign, looking fiercely at Audrea Givens. Just as he'd feared, it looked as if the policeman was having to protect her.

He stared glassy-eyed for a few minutes then read the caption directly below it. "'TEACHER LIVID OVER LOW PAY!' Mr. John Allan admitted that he was 'a frustrated professional that's been pushed to the breaking point by the public's indifference.' He also admitted that he was 'tired of empty promises that evaporate when the public has to pay the bills'!"

"Gee, that's pretty strong," Steve said with surprise. "I thought you took a more middle-of-the-road stance."

John looked up, his eyes blazing. "I do! Those aren't my words. Those are the words of that reporter!"

"Oh."

"This is untenable! The whole town will see this and think that all I care about is the money!" He slapped the paper with the back of his hand. "Look at it! I would never threaten young Audrea or any other student. I was disgusted over that stupid sign Calvin gave me."

"Calvin's sign? Ah . . . I thought you could spell better than that."

"This isn't funny, Steve."

"I'm sorry." He held his hands up in a conciliatory fashion. "Call the newspaper editor up and demand a retraction."

"I will, but do you know where they print the retractions? On the last page, under the farm market report. Nobody is going to see it but the area pig farmers!"

"Okay, demand one of those platforms on the editorial page. You know, where they let the cranks, uh, I mean, concerned citizens, write in and express their views."

John frowned. His friend's slip about cranks was right on the nose. Most people who did take the time to write in, usually wrote about some wacky thing like outlawing skate boards or spotting yellow-bellied sapsuckers in the city park.

"Do it, John," Steve urged. "Also send in a nice picture where you're not so . . . intense."

John wadded up the newspaper and tossed it into the trash can.

"All right. It might undo a little of the damage. I am going to call Audrea's family, though. If I don't explain personally, they may never let her into my class again."

"Good. Really, John, people have a very high opinion of you in this town. They know you, they trust you. They know where you stand. Shoot, you've been teaching for years, decades even. You've taught people's children, their parents, their grandparents . . ."

"Hardy-har. Stop before I feed Teddy your breakfast." John looked uncomfortable as he glanced at the clock. "By the way, aren't you going to be late for work?"

Steve grinned at him sheepishly. He shrugged.

"I've been doing a lot of thinking. I didn't cross the picket line out of any great convictions. It wasn't because I believed the strike was totally wrong. I crossed the picket line for the money, pure and simple."

"And?"

"I have to live in this town. There's more at stake than just money. I realized that when the line of guys was stretched in front of my car yesterday. They were striking for money, sure, but also for better working conditions for themselves and the students. I'll be striking today too. I don't agree with everything the union does, but I also don't want to be the kind of person whose only motivation in life is making money."

John nodded then said, "There are no easy answers in this."

"There seldom is in anything."

24

Standing in the picket line that day was an awful situation. Having Steve shoulder to shoulder with him made John feel a lot better. Even though Steve's constant fidgeting was starting to get on his nerves, he had been glad to see that Steve was readily accepted by the other striking teachers. Even Calvin had been unusually gracious, allowing that everyone was entitled to "make a complete and total idiot of himself once in a while." Steve had taken that little zing with good humor, knowing how much worse it all could have been.

As John tried to keep his mind occupied during the tedious hours of standing, he found his thoughts kept returning to Agnes. He wondered what had happened to her yesterday. What could her message have been? Maybe he could drive over to the Goodwill Store today. What if she wasn't there? Worse yet, what if that sweet little old lady was there? Reading the Bible was one thing, but he certainly didn't want to engage in any discussion about Jesus Christ.

He had to ask himself why he felt that way. After all, he'd even prayed a couple of times in the last few days. He thought about that for a moment. Praying to God was hard

191

enough, but when he thought about Him as Jesus . . . it was like calling someone by his first name when you really weren't sure you wanted to get that familiar.

Jesus—he felt himself shy away from that name without really understanding why. John had never been a man given to cursing, but even in his worse moments of anger or stress, that name had never crossed his lips. There was something about it that he couldn't take lightly.

"Steve, do you go to church?" he asked suddenly, surprising himself as well as his friend.

"What?" He blinked a few times before answering. "Uh, no. I don't. We send the kids to Sunday school though."

"Why?"

"Huh?"

"Why do you send the children if you don't go?"

"I don't know," he said shrugging. "The kids seem to like it. They say they have a lot of fun. I guess I'd go too if I got free cookies and punch. I'd much rather be coloring pictures with the kids than listening to those long, dry sermons of that preacher. How boring."

"My wife's church was never boring. She really loved it. She was there every time the door was open. She'd rather go to church than anything you could name. I only went a couple of times, but the sermons certainly weren't dry."

"Oh," Steve didn't know what to say. He couldn't tell if he was more surprised by John talking about his wife or about church. Both subjects had been strictly off limits for all the years Steve had known the man.

"Where do your children go to Sunday school?"

"Glendale First Community Church. It's big enough to have buses. We just wash the little kiddies up and shove 'em out the door. The church does the rest. It's not a bad arrangement. Sort of like babysitting with free delivery."

"What do they teach your children in Sunday school?"

"What? Uh, Sunday school stuff, I suppose. Bible stories . . . though occasionally the kids will come home spouting off about rain forests and endangered species. I think their teacher is politically correct in a big way. My youngest was having a fit over the fur collar on Carol's coat. He must have picked that up from his Sunday school teacher. My wife and I are healthy carnivores from 'way back."

"Linda was a Sunday school teacher. She took it pretty seriously. She'd start working on her Sunday school lesson a good week in advance. She'd always try everything out on me," John sighed. "Poor Linda, she was never pushy. But I can see now how badly she wanted to convert me."

Steve had absolutely no idea what to say. This whole conversation was coming at him from left field. He soon saw, though, that John wasn't really expecting a response. He was looking off into the distance, lost in thought.

For the rest of the afternoon, John didn't mention his wife or church again. But often he would stand and look so pensive that Steve wondered if he weren't thinking of those very things.

Later that night at home, John picked up the Bible from its place before Linda's picture.

"I wouldn't listen to you, Linda." He held the Bible up to the picture as if she could see it—a curiously sentimental gesture, totally out of character for him. "Maybe I'm ready to listen now."

John sat back on the bed, inviting the amazed Teddy to jump up beside him. The bed had been strictly off limits for the length of Teddy's short life. It was a measure of how glad John was to have the dog back that he would be so lax about his own house rules.

Teddy didn't have to be asked twice. With his usual grace he leaped up and landed in the middle of John's stomach.

"Oof! Now that you've sped up the digestive process of my dinner, settle down and let me read."

Teddy obeyed with the greatest contentment, watching as John opened the Bible to the Book of Exodus.

John began to read of the affliction of the Israelites. With real dismay he read of the edict that condemned all the male babies to death. He had never known of such things being in the Bible. He read with fascination as one mother was able to save her male baby from death. John learned that the child's name was Moses, a name he was familiar with in vague terms.

As John read on into the night, he saw that there had been no happenstance in Moses being saved from death. Moses had gone on to be raised by the very rulers who had oppressed and killed his people. He had gone on to lead his people out of bondage. Again, there had been a plan.

As John got ready for bed that night, he kept thinking of Moses' father. He was scarcely mentioned. How must it have felt to know your own son was being raised by your enemies? To know your child had been adopted by those you hated most? If Moses had been about eighty when he led the Israelites out, his father had probably been long dead, dead before he could see deliverance.

John got between the sheets, thinking of this father who had died nearly four thousand years ago. A father who had died never knowing the reason he had lost his son. He wondered if the man had become bitter. Had the man been comforted by his belief in God, or did he feel God had let him down? The father had never known it, but there had been a reason for him losing his son, a wonderful reason that had saved thousands from slavery. There had been a plan.

He lay for sometime in the darkness, thinking. Linda had loved God so much, yet she had lost her child and her life. Could there have been any reason at all? Any sort of purpose to it?

What a wonderful person she had been. Kind, thoughtful, so loving. If there was a God, could He have been untouched by Linda's spiritual devotion? Would He have allowed her to die so easily?

What was the verse that the little old lady had quoted at the store? Something about God loving us while we were still sinners? If He could love sinners, how much more must He have loved someone like Linda?

For fifteen years John had asked why. Why had his wife and unborn child died? He still couldn't imagine any reason for it, but for the first time he saw that there just might be an answer to his question.

When John awoke the next morning he decided to play hooky. Surely he could be excused from that awful picket line for one day. He thought his time would be better spent writing out an editorial platform for the city paper.

He spent the better part of the morning laboring over his old computer. He remembered the saying, "Writing is easy, you just sit in front of your typewriter and open a vein." He smiled at the truth of it, as he stared at the flickering screen of his monitor. Finally, John decided just to pour his feelings out, a very hard thing for him. He wrote of his love for teaching, for young people. How incredibly fulfilling and frustrating teaching could be. He felt he spoke for most teachers when he wrote of how little concern he had for politics and programs, he only asked for just enough resources to properly educate his students.

After straining his writing through every grammatical sieve he could think of, John printed it out. He was satisfied. He hoped everyone who had seen that terrible piece on the front page would take the time to read this platform.

The ringing phone interrupted his thoughts. John quickly picked it up, hoping to hear the voice of Agnes. He was dismayed by the sound of a tentative male voice.

"Uh, Mr. Allan?"

"Yes?" John answered, not succeeding in hiding his disappointment.

"Uh, maybe this isn't a good time."

"Time for what? Who is this?" he asked rather shortly.

"Oh, I'm sorry! This is Evans Fred. No! I mean Fred Evans!"

John sighed, shaking his head before he answered, "Fred, I'm the one who should apologize. You always seem to catch me at my worst."

"Oh, that's okay. I've gotten used to it. No! I mean, I mean, I didn't mean that!"

John smiled to himself. He could practically feel Fred's misery coming through the phone.

"It's all right, son. I do know what you mean. In fact I almost followed you into church Sunday to apologize for my rudeness, but I was just too stubborn."

"Really?"

"Really. Now what can I do for you?"

"Yeah, well, I just wondered if you still wanted to get together for a pick-up game at noon?"

John stared at his watch, trying to think of some plausible excuse. Playing basketball with a Pentecostal preacher and a zealous Christian like Fred? What a thought!

He was silent just a little too long.

"Of course, if you have other plans . . ." Fred began graciously enough to make John feel guilty.

"No, no. I was wondering, though, how it would work with three players. What if I grab Steve Brooks to even things out?" John would feel a lot better having his comical friend there, keeping everything light.

"Great idea!" the young man enthused.

"It's going on ten now," John told him. "I have to run an errand, then I'll pick up Steve and meet you at the Y."

"Sure thing! Reverend Benning and I are looking forward to it. See you later, Mr. Allan."

"Goodbye, Fred."

Yes, I imagine you and Reverend Benning are looking forward to it, John thought to himself as he went to get his coat. However, with Steve there, I doubt there'll be too much evangelizing.

As John walked into the bedroom to get his keys, he happened to glance at the picture of Linda with the Bible before it. He paused a moment in his thoughts.

"I promise to be polite," he told the picture. "Maybe I can even stop making Fred so nervous around me."

25

After John dropped his article off at the newspaper, he swung by the school looking for Steve. Steve was hard to miss. In the long line of sullen-faced strikers holding sober placards, Steve was wearing a loopy smile, proudly holding a sign that read, "Will Work for Food."

John laughed as he pulled his van up to the sidewalk and rolled the window down. "Steve! What are you doing with that sign?"

Steve looked to his right, then to his left, answering in a loud stage whisper, "Making Calvin mad!"

The strikers on either side of him laughed as he jauntily walked up to the van. Good old Steve, John thought to himself.

"You look like you need some exercise," John told him.

"I do?"

"Yes. Get in and we'll go play some basketball."

"But mother told me not to accept rides with strangers."

"It'll make Calvin mad if you leave."

"I'm coming, I'm coming!"

John looked Steve over as he got into the van. "I knew

you'd be wearing a sweat suit. Tell me do you own any clothes that aren't made out of jersey?"

Steve ignored him as he busily fiddled with the radio. After moving the dial from John's favorite classical station to a heavy rock radio station, he leaned back with a sigh into the seat.

"Ah, this is the life. Cranking up the tunes in a really cool, sporty quarter-ton van. You know John, if this strike continues you could pick up some money hauling logs for the lumber yard. Or you could rent the back to a family of illegal aliens. What a big van!"

John smiled, glad his friend was in such good spirits. It was just what he wanted. Who could talk about such serious things as church with a wiseacre like Steve around?

"Where are we playing, the park?" Steve asked.

"No, the YMCA," John said as he pulled into the street.

"I'm not a member; you'll have to pay my way, you know," he said brightly.

"Don't I always?"

"True. Whew, electric windows!" Steve began to play with the window button.

"Stop that. Fred Evans will be there."

"Really? He's a nice kid." Steve went back to the radio, changing the station to country and western, then back to rock again.

"Stop that. He's bringing a friend too."

"Oh? Another student teacher?" he pulled down the visor fascinated by the lighted mirror. He began to play with the on-and-off switch.

"Stop that! No, it's his minister."

Steve stopped. "We're playing basketball with a minister?"

"Yes, Fred asked and I didn't know how to say no."

Steve sat back in his seat, suddenly serious.

"He seemed like a nice man," John commented.

"You've met him?"

"Yes, the other day when I was looking for Teddy."

"Oh," Steve made no other sound for the next few streets.

John finally looked over at him, concerned that his talkative friend was so quiet.

"John, this is basketball! What if I slip and say something I shouldn't?"

"You never curse anyway."

"I know but . . . things get rough sometimes. What if I accidentally hack him? Can you go to hell for fouling a minister?"

"Sure, it's the Eleventh Commandment. Come on Steve, you're not exactly some inner-city thug playing hoops for drug money."

"I know, I know." He ran a hand through his hair nervously. "But gee whiz, a minister! I wonder if I should say 'gee whiz'?"

John pulled into the YMCA parking lot, totally dismayed at his friend. He had not expected this reaction. Steve got out of the van like a man going to the dentist for a root canal. He certainly wasn't going to be any help. He looked like some lost soul that really needed preaching to.

They made a very quiet pair as they entered the building and went to the front desk. After paying a small fee for Steve, they went straight to the gym. John saw that Fred and his pastor were already there, throwing some practice shots. He also saw with some surprise that they were the only ones there. The huge gym was empty except for the four men.

"Hello!" Fred called, his voice echoing in the empty building. "Hello, Mr. Brooks, it's good to see you again," he continued as he walked towards them. "I guess it hasn't been that long, but it seems long in a way . . ."

John could see that Fred was just as nervous as Steve.

201

Well, this should be a fun afternoon, he thought sarcastically.

Of the four, Reverend Benning seemed to be the only relaxed one among them. He had dressed casually in jeans and sweat shirt, giving him a much different look than the suit he'd had on Sunday. He didn't seem nearly as intimidating as John had remembered.

"Do you believe this? Fred and I couldn't get over how empty the Y was today. They told us at the desk they had never seen the place like this," he said to John and Steve.

Both men just shook their heads. There was an awkward silence.

"Yes, well, let's play ball," Reverend Benning said with some amusement, understanding their silence. He'd seen it many times before. "So you're the high school basketball coach?"

"Yes, sir," Steve answered like a schoolboy.

Yes, sir? Sir? John couldn't believe his friend.

"Good!" Reverend Benning chortled. "Then you're on my side! Sorry, gentlemen," he turned to John and Fred. "But I like to win."

John found himself smiling. "Then why did you pick Steve?" he asked in the same bantering style. "Come on, Fred, let's show 'em."

In a few moments they had a nice game going. They played full court, full out. John soon found himself lost in the game. It wasn't long before he was able to forget he was playing against a minister. He was playing against a really good basketball player.

By the end of the second quarter John saw that Steve was relaxing more. He was probably relieved he wasn't playing against Reverend Benning. They stopped to take a short break to rest.

"Are you all right?" Fred asked his pastor solicitously.

"Sure, never felt better."

John looked up in surprise at Fred's question. The

minister was about John's age and seemed to be the picture of health. In fact, he'd been giving everyone a real run for his money.

Reverend Benning caught John's curiosity. "I had a kidney transplant two years ago," he said matter-of-factly.

Both Steve and John looked at him in astonishment.

"What? How . . . how can you play basketball?" Steve spluttered. "Here, do you need to sit down or something?"

"No, I'm fine really," Reverend Benning said laughing.

"You seem so healthy. I've known a few transplant patients and they certainly weren't able to play basketball," John commented.

"I know," Reverend Benning nodded his head. "I had wonderful doctors and a great surgeon, but I feel the Lord has touched me in a miraculous way."

Steve looked uncomfortable and bent to tie his shoe. John however found that he was fascinated.

"I don't know a great deal about kidney transplants, but you must have been very sick," John said.

Fred nodded his head at this point. "He was. It was awful. Everyone was afraid that we would lose him."

Reverend Benning smiled gratefully at Fred, then gave him a hearty pat on the back. "Yes, I had congestive heart failure at one point, but I had a whole church full of people like Fred praying for me. God pulled me through."

"God must have had a plan for your life," John said quietly.

The three men looked at him in surprised silence. John was pretty surprised himself. After a long moment, Reverend Benning spoke up. "Why, yes. I believe that too."

John just nodded, embarrassed. He picked up the basketball from the floor. "Well, if everyone's ready, let's finish this game."

They played the last two quarters in relative silence,

everyone pondering John's surprising comment. John was wondering where in the world it had come from. The other three men had assumed John was something close to an atheist. They all wondered what could have caused him to say such a thing.

After learning of the minister's kidney transplant, John had curbed his usual aggressive play. He was worried he might jostle the man or injure him in some way. It cost them a few points, which cost them the game.

Afterwards Reverend Benning slapped Steve a strong high five. "Yes!" he exulted, then he turned to John. "Tell me, did you back off just because you knew about my transplant?" he asked accusingly.

"Oh, I . . ." John trailed off.

"I thought so. I want a rematch, then. I won't be coddled."

A grin etched across John's face. I like this man, he thought to himself. I like his attitude. "All right, then. Next week, same time?" he asked.

"Great, Fred? Steve?"

Fred only nodded, but Steve looked unsure.

"Well, if the strike's still going on," he temporized. "I'll let you know."

As the men picked up their jackets, Reverend Benning spoke to John quietly. "That was an interesting comment you made, about God having a plan. When I would spend those long hours on the dialysis machine, I kept thinking that there was a purpose to it all. You and I must think alike."

John really doubted that but he didn't say so. He shouldered his jacket on, making sure there was a nice sharp crease in the lapels. He looked up to see Reverend Benning was watching him, expecting a response.

"I've been glancing at the Bible a few times this week, just skimming," John shrugged, trying to sound nonchalant. "I happened to notice in the first two books that there was an underlying theme, that God always had a plan for the main characters' lives."

"That's pretty good for just skimming. A lot of people miss that point," Reverend Benning said. "No matter what people believe, the Bible is a beautiful piece of literature. It's a shame more people don't study it. It has everything—history, poetry, allegories, even songs."

Shaking his head, John admitted, "I've begun to feel I should know more about it, just from a literary point of view, of course."

"Of course."

John cocked an eyebrow, but there was no irony in the other man's voice. He didn't seem inclined to pursue the subject either. Apparently there would be no preaching today. John was grateful.

"Good game, see you next week." Reverend Benning smiled and turned to leave with Fred.

Fred, suddenly remembering something, turned back to John. "Oh, Mr. Allan, I wanted to tell you, I saw Clark this morning. He seems to be doing much better. His attitude is really improving."

"That's wonderful, but how on earth did you get in to see him?"

Fred shook his head. "I just did. I've been going by every day. I never had any problems."

"Really? What about his mother?"

"She was never there."

"Aren't you the lucky one. He's doing better? That's great; he has a lot going for him. I wonder what's turning him around?"

"Well, we've been doing a little talking."

"Oh, what about?"

Fred paused for a minute, not sure of how to proceed. He smiled and said gently, "I've been trying to show him that God has a plan for his life."

26

After John took Steve home, he found himself driving to the Goodwill Store. He just had to find out if Agnes was working there. If she wasn't, he could listen to a few more Bible verses from that little old lady. It would be a small price to pay. Maybe she'd even give him Agnes's phone number.

He suddenly remembered with dismay that he hadn't taken a shower at the Y. He'd always been too fussy to use public facilities. He'd planned on going straight home and showering there. Now, how could he possibly see Agnes after two hours of basketball?

His desire to see Agnes was pretty strong, but his natural fastidiousness won out and he hurried home to clean up. An hour later he was back in the van and on his way to the Goodwill Store. He had dressed carefully, wearing his best white turtleneck shirt with his tweed suit. He hoped she'd notice.

He pushed the front door of the shop open, expecting Agnes would be working today. He was disappointed to see an elderly man this time, working behind the counter.

"Hello, I wonder if Agnes is working today?"

The man looked up suspiciously. His bright blue eyes

207

peered out under an enormously bushy pair of white eyebrows. He didn't return John's smile.

"She was. But she left a short while ago."

Of course!

"I'm . . . I'm a friend of hers. I don't suppose you could give me her phone number?"

"Nope."

"Oh, well, all right," John sighed and left the building.

All dressed up and no place to go, he thought to himself as he got into the van. He thought of Fred's discussion of Clark. So Fred had been preaching at him, eh? Maybe he'd better go over there and make sure Fred wasn't coming on too strong.

As he drove across town, John had to ask himself what would be wrong with Fred talking to Clark about God. After all, he certainly hadn't had any great gems of wisdom to offer the boy. Still, there was the teacher-student relationship. It made John very uneasy to have Fred forcing his religion on a student, especially if he was in the hospital, a captive audience.

The great gray nurse wasn't standing guard that day. Instead a very pleasant-looking black woman smiled at John as soon as he approached the reception desk of the Rehab Ward.

"Good afternoon. May I help you?"

"Yes ma'am. I'd like to see Clark Nelson."

"Of course." She rose and spoke into the intercom, "Visitor for Clark."

The door was promptly opened by a chubby little man about John's age. He offered John another smile.

"Right this way. It's nice for these kids to have visitors."

John nodded, glad to have come when these two pleasant people were on shift.

Clark looked up as John entered his room. The boy had unbraided his two dreadlocks so he now looked out at the world through a shaggy mop of brightly colored hair.

208

"'Lo, Mr. A," he said calmly, his mouth lifting in a crooked grin.

"Hello, Clark. What happened to Godzilla and King Kong?" John asked as he took a chair.

"I guess they only work the weekend shift. Can't say that I'm sorry."

"No, I don't suppose you are. How's the arm?"

Clark raised his heavy cast a few inches. "Better. Itches like crazy. Do you know which hand I write with?"

"No, I don't."

"Good." Clark moved the cast again. "It's this one," he said slyly. "Guess there's no more homework for me, huh?"

"Why am I suspicious? I'm sure Audrea will be glad to take notes for you. When do you get out?"

"Saturday."

"Great." John wasn't sure how to ask the next question. "Is everything . . . going to work out for you? I mean, you're going to be all right?"

"Yeah, Mom's thrown her weight around so I only have to come in for counseling once a week. My folks make some pretty big donations to this hospital." He shrugged. "Nobody's going to ask too many questions."

"That's good, I guess," John said with concern. "But what are you going to do, son? What are you going to change so that you don't end up back here?"

Clark looked away. For the first time since he'd known him, John saw the boy was actually embarrassed. "I've been talking a lot to Mr. Evans."

John shifted in his chair. "I hope he hasn't been preaching at you."

"I thought he was at first, but it's so natural with him, talking about God and stuff, that I don't think he can really help it."

"True, but—"

"And you know, Mr. A? Some of the stuff he said, it helped. It helped a lot."

"Well, that's good of course, Clark. But I still think there has to be a clear separation—"

"I never thought anything mattered," Clark interrupted again. "I never thought anything I did made any difference to anybody."

"Oh, son! It matters a great deal! You have so many talents, so much to offer the world."

"Yeah? Thanks, but I dunno, I just never felt that way. Until lately, that is. When you hear Mr. Evans talk, things make sense." Clark gave him another lopsided grin. "I kinda thought he was pretty goofy at first. He's all right, though. He's really okay."

John didn't know what to say. The boy certainly seemed in much better spirits than when he'd last seen him. If Fred was helping, who was he to argue?

"What does he talk about?" John asked.

"Jesus stuff. But not like you'd think. Not like some TV evangelist guy. It's more like Jesus is this real person that Mr. E sees every day. When Mr. E talks about Jesus, you kinda start thinking He's down in the parking lot, waiting in Mr. E's car."

John smiled at the thought.

"Apparently you haven't seen the inside of Mr. Evans's car," he said dryly.

"Pretty bad, huh?" Clark asked grinning. "Anyway, if Jesus is the way Mr. E says, I dunno, it'd be pretty nice."

"I suppose . . . still there's just so many questions," John admitted candidly.

"Yeah, but like Mr. E says, you can listen to the radio even if you don't know how it works."

"That's pretty good."

"Yeah, Mr. E is always saying stuff like that. Kinda surprising, isn't he?"

"Yes, yes, he is." John thought it was a good time to change the subject. "Have you seen Audrea lately?"

"Why? Are you going to ask her how to spell 'learning'?"

210

"Noo . . . You've seen that picture in the paper?" he groaned.

"Who hasn't?"

"I have to talk to Audrea. It's not the way it looks. Mr. Loring had just shoved that sign in my hands. I wasn't mad at Audrea at all. I was irritated with Mr. Loring."

"Don't worry, Mr. A. She figured it was something like that. Besides, it'll give us ammunition for the rest of the year."

John leaned back in his chair and looked at Clark through narrowed eyes. "Ammunition, young man?" he asked in his deepest voice. "What did you mean by that?"

"How will you ever be able to give us a spelling test again?"

"Ah, but you see, I didn't make that sign. Mr. Loring did."

Both their smiles dried up as Clark's mother walked into the room. Today, she was wearing a deep brown leather coat with a soft white fur collar framing her face. Her pretty face fell into hard lines when she saw John. She didn't speak.

He sighed and rose from his chair. He nodded politely to Mrs. Nelson. "Hello, Mrs. Nelson. I was just leaving."

She nodded a fraction of an inch.

"Take care, Clark. I hope to see you back in class soon."

"Now how is that supposed to happen, Mr. Allan?" Mrs. Nelson asked acidly. "Your strike has pretty much put Clark's education on hold."

"Mom!" Clark protested.

"It's true, Clark. It's all very well for him to waltz in here acting all concerned. But I guess we know how you really feel, don't we? After that picture in the paper and your little pithy comments. I guess we know where your priorities lie."

"Ah, Mom, everyone knows—"

John held up his hand, looking steadily at Mrs. Nelson. He wondered what it'd be like living with such an unpleasant woman. "That's all right, Clark. I'm sure your mother knows how badly the press can mislead people."

"Do I? Well, I think you should know, Mr. Nelson and I are looking into enrolling Clark in a private school where he'll get a quality education."

"What? What's this? You can't be serious!" Clark sat forward in his bed deeply agitated.

Mrs. Nelson faltered for a moment, looking with concern at Clark. Her face hardened as she turned back to John. "See what you've done! I hadn't meant to say anything yet."

John shook his head. "Mrs. Nelson, are you sure about this? Clark needs to deal with his problems where he is. Changing locations won't solve anything."

"I don't see that it's any of your business," she returned coldly.

John looked helplessly at Clark, who was staring at his mother with pure hatred. "You can't make me go!" The boy spoke loudly with great conviction. "I'll run away!"

"Clark! Don't you threaten me! I'll—" Mrs. Nelson broke off to snap at John. "Would you please go?"

The little orderly stood in the doorway, concerned by the sound of raised voices. Mrs. Nelson tried to regain her composure, while John nodded to him.

"I'm leaving, I'm leaving," John told him before he turned to place his hand on Clark's shoulder. "Please don't do anything rash, son."

The orderly followed John into the hallway and towards the exit. "It's like this everytime his mother comes," the man muttered.

"I'm not surprised."

"But that other visitor, that real tall young fella, he can get Clark to smilin' and laughin' faster than anything."

As soon as John went home that evening, he began to

look through the phone book for Fred's number. Upon finding it, he dialed quickly, hoping to find the young man home.

"Hello?"

"Fred, I'm so glad you're there. This is John Allan."

"Hi, Mr. Allan," Fred said with surprise. "What can I do for you?"

"It's not for me, Fred. I've just left Clark. He seemed to be doing better just like you said, then his mother came in and upset him. She's threatening to put him in a private school, so now he's threatening to run away."

"Oh, no."

"Fred, Clark seems to have really taken to you . . ." John slowed as he swallowed his pride. "I have to admit, you've been able to reach him where I couldn't."

"It's not me, Mr. Allan."

"Whatever it is, I was wondering if you could go over and talk to him this evening. His mother will probably be gone by then."

"Sure, I'll get right over there."

"Thank you, Fred," John said with humble gratitude. "Thank you very much."

"No problem . . . uh, Mr. Allan?"

"Yes?"

"I don't know if this is a good time, I was going to ask you something this afternoon, but I didn't want to seem pushy or anything. I know how you feel about—"

"Fred?"

"Yes."

"I really make you nervous, don't I?" John asked kindly, determined to make amends with this good-hearted young man.

"Well, uh, in a way I guess. Not that it's your fault. I know I talk a lot and put my foot in my mouth a lot."

"I'll tell you what. Go ahead and ask me your question. I appreciate so much what you've done with Clark

213

that, no matter what it is, I promise to answer politely and to grant any favors that you could name!"

"Really?"

"Upon my honor!"

"Great! See, my church is having revival services this Sunday, and I was wondering if you'd like to come."

27

Feeling like a condemned man, John worried for the next two days. He couldn't believe he had promised to go to church with Fred. Not just to church either, but a revival service. He might not have minded Reverend Benning's sermon too much. He seemed like a pretty normal man. But there was to be a special evangelist Sunday, probably some wild-eyed zealot they brought in for special occasions. John shuddered.

He considered dragging Steve along for moral support but quickly rejected that idea. Steve certainly hadn't been much help the other day. He reminded himself that he hadn't really needed Steve. Both Reverend Benning and Fred had been very pleasant.

Maybe I'm overreacting, he thought at different times. I can just go and sit in the back, do poor Fred a favor. The music should be nice. Such reasonable thoughts didn't last long though. He'd soon get a vivid picture of some Billy Sunday character leaping over the pews to grab him by the lapels and shake the sin right out of him.

By Saturday John had worked himself into such a state that he awoke with only one thought. He'd have to call Fred and offer some plausible excuse for not coming.

He hated to disappoint the boy. After all, he'd been so nice about dropping everything and going to see Clark. Then again, Fred had gone on at some length about John meeting his mother.

As John lay in bed that morning he had to smile to himself. Fred was probably trying to fix up his old widowed mother. She was probably some ancient thing with her gray hair pulled back in a severe bun. He self-consciously ran his hand over his smooth scalp. Because of his baldness, young people always thought he was much older than his forty years. Fred must assume John could keep his mother company in her golden years, reading her Scripture while she knitted Bible bookmarks.

John glanced up at Linda's picture on the bureau. Was he being fair? Linda had been a vibrant attractive woman. Why did he keep thinking of Christians as eccentrics? Linda certainly hadn't been. Fred, for all his nervousness, was a very nice young man. Reverend Benning seemed to be quite pleasant too. Then there was Agnes. She must be some sort of Christian to talk about the Bible the way she did.

He sighed when he thought about Agnes. He'd only seen her once, only talked to her once on the phone. Yet she'd occupied his thoughts all week. She'd been so maddenly elusive. Should he go back to the Goodwill Store today? What if the other employees thought he was some sort of crazed stalker? If any of them had seen that picture in the newspaper they would surely think he was unhinged. John sat up in bed. Was that it? Had Agnes seen the picture and purposely been avoiding him all week? Why had he thought she would laugh it off? She didn't know him. No, she'd think he was some awful jerk.

Teddy leaped into his lap, interrupting his thoughts. Once he'd let the dog on the bed, he'd had an awful time restoring his old training.

"Ted, get down," John said firmly. "You know better."

Teddy licked his face.

"Now I mean it, get down."

John sighed again and gently scooped the dog up. "I wish everyone felt about me the way you did."

John spent the rest of the morning trying to come up with some plausible excuses to tell Fred. He didn't want to lie to the boy. Still, he just froze at the thought of going to church tomorrow.

By late afternoon he'd finally settled on something halfway reasonable when the phone rang. He hoped it was Fred, so he could get it over with.

"Hello?"

"John, Steve here. Just read your platform article in the paper. It was really good."

"And?"

"And what?"

"You paid me a compliment, I'm waiting for the punchline."

"Well, I like that! I try to be sincere, to take things seriously and do I get any credit? Nooo . . ."

"I'm sorry, Steve."

"That's okay. I really was impressed. You even spelled everything correctly."

"That's more like it."

"Right, I'll see you first thing Monday morning."

After John hung up, he reached to dial Fred, but the phone rang again before he could pick up the receiver.

"Hello?"

"Allan? Loring here. I wanted to tell you I've been getting a lot of positive feedback about your platform in the paper."

"Really?"

"Yeah, since it came out this morning, people have been talking. You were able to put a lot of our goals into simple enough words for the average person to understand."

"Oh? Uh, thank you." Was that a compliment? John asked himself.

"Things are looking up. The public didn't really believe we'd go on strike, then wham! We did. Then that little editorial of yours showed that we can be reasonable too. The union is talking about waiting a week, then seeing if an emergency levy could be pushed through."

"So soon?"

"Sure. It's getting near the end of the semester. There won't be much point in striking when the kids are on their holiday vacations. Plus, if we're out too long, the parents know it could really hurt their kids' education." Calvin had a gloating tone that disgusted John.

"I thought it was for the children's education that we went out on strike in the first place."

"Oh, yeah, of course. Well, keep up the good work, John."

"Right. Goodbye, Calvin."

John decided to give Fred one more try. Again, the phone rang before he could pick up the receiver to dial.

"Hello!" he said with a decided grumpiness.

"Uh, hello. Mr. Allan," said a familiar meek voice. "Bad timing again?"

John groaned inwardly. "Fred. You know I really am a nice person, despite all evidence to the contrary."

"Oh, I know it! Even when you're so . . ." Fred thankfully stopped himself in time. "Anyway, I wanted to tell you how much I enjoyed your platform editorial in the paper. I showed it to my mom. She thought it was great. She said you must be a very sensitive person."

"How nice," John said pleasantly, wondering all the while how much Fred was going to push his mother on him.

"I really can't wait for you to meet her tomorrow. I mean . . ." Fred paused as if searching for the right words. "You both have a lot in common, you both love literature."

Right, the only things she probably reads beside the Bible are cookbooks and the back of cereal boxes, John couldn't help but think. "About tomorrow, Fred . . ."

"Oh yeah, I wanted to tell you. I spoke to Clark a couple of times. I think he's going to be okay. He's getting used to the idea of a private school. I pointed out that it might be good for him to have a complete change."

"Well, that's true," John admitted, slowly.

"I hope you don't mind, but when I told him you were going to be at my church tomorrow, he said he'd come too. He'll be leaving for his new school on Monday and he wanted to say goodbye." Fred paused again before continuing. "Uh, I guess his mom wasn't too keen on his coming over and seeing you again. I mean, I didn't lie or anything, I just didn't tell her you'd be at my church."

"Oh." Now what? John asked himself. How can I miss a chance to say goodbye to that poor boy?

"Do you think I was being dishonest, Mr. Allan? I felt so sorry for Clark. Plus, I have to admit, it won't hurt him to take in a church service."

"It was a tough call, Fred. Your heart's in the right place. I think you did the right thing."

"Thanks. Well, I'll see you at ten tomorrow!"

"Right, ten o'clock."

Feeling like a noose was tightening around his throat John hung up the phone. He spent the rest of the afternoon and evening with a feeling of anxiety hanging over him like a black shroud. He couldn't believe the feelings of dread that were welling up in him.

It had become a nightly habit for John to read the Bible before he went to sleep. He told himself it was only a scholarly study to broaden his literature base. He was unable to admit to himself how much he had begun to look forward to his nightly Bible reading. He found it very comforting.

He almost skipped it that night, though. It reminded

him too much of the church he would be attending tomorrow. He sat on the bed for a long time, just holding the Bible in his lap. What on earth am I afraid of? John asked himself. Afraid of becoming a Christian? Afraid of becoming a religious fanatic?

His eyes drifted to the picture of Linda. No, that wasn't it. Becoming a Christian had only expanded her already good qualities. Then what was he so afraid of?

The word "hope" wafted through his mind. He sat a little straighter, suddenly understanding himself. He clutched the Bible as if it were a lifeline and shut his eyes.

"Uh, you know . . ." he began in the same uncertain way he always did when he prayed. "I didn't have any hope for fifteen years. I didn't have anything to look forward to. I see now how bad it was, but I got used to it," he shrugged. "Things are starting to look up, to make sense. What if . . ." he trailed off for a moment. "What if I start getting involved, start believing like Linda did, only to have the bottom fall out again? I don't think I could stand it. I'm afraid," he whispered to the floor.

John felt that he uttered the most awkward and feeble prayers ever said. He wasn't even sure why he was doing it. Yet invariably, he always felt a little better. That night was no different. He took a deep breath and opened his eyes. Strange, the room even seemed brighter.

He leaned back and propped up the pillows, preparing to read. He had worked up to the Book of Joshua, and he was almost immediately struck by Joshua 1:9:

"Have not I commanded thee? Be strong and of a good courage: be not afraid, neither be thou dismayed: for the LORD thy God is with thee whithersoever thou goest."

John smiled to himself. He reread the verse many times. He decided to stop at that verse, wanting it to be the last thing he read before he went to sleep. As he reached out to turn off the light, Teddy leaped on the bed beside him.

28

First of all, John awoke much later than usual that Sunday morning. He couldn't believe it. He normally was up at 6:00 AM with or without his alarm clock. The clock read almost 9:00.

Then after a mad scramble to get Teddy back into the house and fed, John broke two shoelaces. He was sorely tempted not to go at all, but he kept picturing Clark's sad face.

It was nearly 10:00 when John parked his van and hurried up the church steps. He'd planned on taking a seat in the back, but all the rear rows were filled. Almost towards the front he saw an empty space beside a nicely dressed young man. John hesitated. It was too close to the podium, but a smiling usher pointed towards the spot as if they'd saved it just for him. John gave him a weak smile in return and trudged up the aisle. The first strains of the opening hymn were just beginning to play as he sat down.

Fred suddenly appeared at his elbow.

"Hi! Mr. Allan. Boy, it's packed today! Mom and I are in the back on the other side. We'll talk after service. I'm glad to see you got a seat by Clark," he said before bounding off to the other side of the church.

221

John looked around in amazement. Clark was sitting next to him, but not any version of the Clark he had known. This boy had a trim crew cut (just a little spiked in the front) and a suit with a plain white shirt and tie.

"Clark?" John asked uncertainly.

"'Lo, Mr. A," Clark said, a large smile on his face.

"What's all this? And your hair!"

Clark almost laughed. No matter how strange or bizarre he had worn his hair to school, Mr. Allan had been unfazed. Now he seemed disconcerted to have Clark looking so normal.

"Mr. E's been talking to me about new beginnings. I figured if I went to that private school I'd just be setting myself up, you know, to go in looking like a slacker." Clark looked almost shy as he glanced down at his polished leather shoes. "Maybe if I give 'em a chance they'll give me a chance."

"That's pretty good thinking, son."

"Yeah, well, all teachers aren't as open-minded as you," Clark looked up for a moment, then glanced back down at his shoes. "I always knew I could be myself in your class. You never thought I was a troublemaker, just 'coz of my hair."

"Thank you." John smiled at the boy's bent head, wondering where Clark's self-assuredness had gone or if it had ever been there. "You've always been one of my better students."

Their attention was diverted as the choir walked across the platform. They were being directed by a pretty young woman with light blond hair. John wondered if it was the same girl who had led the youth choir so many years ago. John smiled, thinking how pleased Linda would have been to have seen such a large choir on the platform.

The music was as good as he had remembered. The song had a nice up tempo without sounding too rocky.

John leaned back in his pew. Perhaps he could get through this.

After two songs, Brother Benning walked up to the large wooden lectern in the middle of the platform and smiled at the congregation. "Good morning, everyone! Thank you all for being with us today. We've been having a great week of revival. God has been changing lives and filling people with His Spirit.

"As our evangelist comes, let's all say, 'God bless Brother de Gresroi.'"

Brother Benning then left the lectern to a tall slim man who was quite as bald as John. The evangelist smiled almost shyly at the congregation while he took a pair of bifocals from his pocket.

As the evangelist began to speak John was immediately struck by the man's soft, cultured voice. He had a refined way of talking that was very pleasant to the ears. Because of the man's name, John thought for a few moments that the man had an accent. He didn't. He just had a wonderful command of correct usage and diction.

Perhaps no one else in the congregation could appreciate this as well as John. After a career of hearing incorrect grammar daily, this man was a pure joy to listen to.

It was several minutes before John could shift his attention from how the man was speaking to what he was actually saying. John realized he was familiar with the man's text. He was preaching from the Book of Genesis, the book that John had read through last week.

Brother de Gresroi started at the very beginning with Adam and Eve and the forbidden fruit in the garden. John had wondered about that. Surely, he'd reasoned, wouldn't it have been better to just have left that tree out of the garden? Why even give them a chance to sin?

Brother de Gresroi had an answer to that. When God had created man it wasn't with the thought of creating mindless puppets. He wanted to be loved by choice, not

223

by mandate. How could God have enjoyed any relationship with creatures who had no choice? The forbidden tree represented the free will that everyone has. Sadly, Adam and Eve had chosen wrong.

John found he was spell-bound by this soft-spoken preacher. The man further contended that Eve's first mistake had been relying on her own knowledge rather than faith in God's Word. That pricked John to the heart. John, who thought knowledge to be everything, had to concede the man's point. After all, Eve couldn't have known as much as God, couldn't have known He had a greater purpose in store. By relying solely on her own meager knowledge of the situation, Eve had lost everything.

As the preacher spoke on, John felt hammered by every word. What did he know? What could he possibly understand? Could his little perspective, his small knowledge, match an omnipotent God's?

Sin entered the world by man's choice, the evangelist said. All sin. Sin in every form. Even the sin of a man drunk out of his mind, slamming his car into the car of an expectant mother, John thought to himself.

Then Reverend de Gresroi quoted Romans 5:18: "Therefore as by the offense of one [Adam] judgment came upon all men to condemnation."

There had to be judgment for sin. If God was to be truly pure and holy, He couldn't abide sin in His presence. It began to make sense to John. He had always taught his students to expect consequences for wrong actions. He also began to see that he would have done just what Adam and Eve had done.

As John sat on the soft, padded pew, a very hard thought came to his mind. He was a sinner. He had spent fifteen years—no a lifetime—wondering about God's actions, with never a thought to his own. How could he ever hope to stand in judgment before a holy God? He had never chosen God, never chose to love or serve Him.

What if God chose to reject him? It was a chilling thought.

"But God had a plan," Reverend de Gresroi said. John stared at the man, as if he were a mind reader.

With all the judgments handed out to Adam and Eve, the evangelist began to show there had also been a promise. He then quoted Genesis 3:15:

"And I will put enmity between thee and the woman, and between thy seed and her seed; it shall bruise thy head, and thou shalt bruise his heel."

John had not understood this verse when he read it. But the evangelist made it clear. Even though it seemed the devil had won a victory by getting Adam and Eve to fall, the day would come when the seed, or offspring, of this first couple would defeat sin and the devil. From the very start God had planned a Messiah to save people not only from sin but the judgment that went with it. This Messiah, Jesus Christ, would pay the price of judgment with His own death.

Jesus Christ—there was that name again. John began to feel all broken up inside. There was no getting around it. He would have to deal with the man, the God, who held that name.

Reverend de Gresroi made it sound so sweet. There was someone who loved John. Loved him now, when he was still angry and hurting. There was someone who loved him enough to endure a painful death in order for John not to face the judgment he deserved.

John wanted to be loved. He wanted it so badly. He allowed the last crumbling wall within him to topple over. As the sermon ended and the congregation rose to its feet, Reverend de Gresroi made an invitation. Anyone could know Jesus, anyone at all. Would they come now, to this altar, and meet the Savior who loved them enough to die for them?

Reverend de Gresroi didn't yell, didn't plead. He spoke reasonably, like a man who knew he was making the best offer in the world.

The young blond woman slipped up to the piano and began to play. Softly she began to sing:

When the roll is called up yonder,
When the roll is called up yonder
I'll be there.

John thought of all the roll calls he had taken in his teaching career.

Would, could God be taking a roll call someday? If so would John be marked absent?

John struggled with his pride for a few moments, but he knew from experience what cold comfort pride was. After a few nervous tugs on his lapel, John left his pew and found a spot at the corner of the altar where he could kneel and be nearly hidden by a large potted plant.

Several others were crowding towards the altar, eager to meet Jesus too. John sighed, glad for his relative obscurity. He tried hard to keep his feelings under control, to pray in a dignified manner. He tried. But fifteen years of pain came welling up, washing over his reserves.

He cried. He spoke in broken sentences, trying to convey everything he felt. John heard raised voices all around him, but they seemed very far away. He wanted to know love again. He wanted to know, to feel, the love of this Jesus.

After a short time, John felt a tissue being pushed into his hands. He looked up to see Reverend Benning kneeling beside him.

"Do you believe that you're a sinner?" The preacher asked quietly.

John could only nod.

"Then you must believe that Jesus can also forgive your sins. Do you know what we mean by the baptism of the Holy Ghost?"

"I . . . a little."

"Jesus not only loves you enough to die for you, He loves you enough to live within you and empower you to live for Him. As you begin to praise Him He will fill you with His Spirit."

John didn't pretend to understand everything, but he was as obedient as a little child. As Reverend Benning instructed him he began to raise his hands and praise the Lord. It was probably just as well that he wasn't aware of the small crowd that had gathered behind him, praying as fervently for him as he was for himself.

The more John prayed the better he felt. The dignified English teacher became quite loud as he felt the last vestiges of sorrow and bitterness leave him. He didn't know he could feel such happiness; he wasn't sure he could contain it. Totally unmindful of his surroundings, John leaped up and began to shout. He didn't know what he was shouting, though. It didn't make sense. He couldn't understand the words. He kept shouting anyway. The words, whatever they were, just rolled out of him. He knew semantics well enough to recognize that this wasn't gibberish. He was speaking a fully formed language. But the wonder of it still didn't compare to what was taking place within his soul.

A good while later, John became aware enough of his surroundings to realize that someone was shouting even louder than he was. John opened his eyes to see that Clark was having the exact same experience that he was. John began to weep then. What a merciful God! No, John told himself, what a merciful Jesus! From now on, they were on a first-name basis.

John smiled to himself. When the roll was called up yonder he'd be there!

Epilogue

Wore out with joy, John finally had to stop praising his new friend Jesus. He sat down on the altar, content to watch Clark express all the gratitude that he felt himself.

"I can't tell you how happy I am for you!" a soft feminine voice said behind him.

John whirled around at the sound of the voice. "Agnes!"

Her beautiful green eyes were moist with tears as she nodded her head.

"This . . . you go to this church?" he asked with wonder.

"Yes," she nodded. "Fred and I have gone here for years."

"Fred?" John stood up, realization dawning on him. "You're Fred's mother, the woman he's been wanting me to meet!"

She smiled mischievously.

"Did you know? Did you know I was Fred's supervising teacher?"

"How do you think I got your phone number when I called you?"

John sat down again, embarrassed. "I've been so mean to your son."

"Yes, you have," she said cheerfully.

John raised an eyebrow at that.

"There were a couple of times that I really wanted to tell you off. But Fred liked you so much. Then when I actually met you in the store and realized who you were . . ." she trailed off, embarrassed now too. "Well,

229

anyway, you seemed very nice. Fred and I figured you were grouchy because you were under conviction."

"I felt like you were avoiding me all week. Was it because of how I treated Fred last Sunday?"

"Oh, no," she assured him, blushing. "I . . ."

Whatever she was going to say was lost as Brother Benning and Brother de Gresroi joined them. After a small discussion it was decided that John would be baptized that night at the evening service along with Clark.

John looked over at Clark, who was still worshiping Jesus. He was glad that Clark wouldn't have the wasted years that John had. He was glad that the boy had discovered the plan for his life so much sooner than John had.

But Jesus does have a plan for me! John assured himself gladly. Then, as he looked shyly over at Agnes, he wondered just what all that plan could hold.